CW01271037

'Every punch, every hit... it's a piece of yourself you're leaving behind.'

Echoes of Vengeance

Author's Note

Dear Reader,

Echoes of Vengeance isn't just a story; it is a reflection of my journey through pain, resilience, and search for meaning after others broke me. The plot and characters, despite being fictitious, have their roots in the experiences that shaped me.

I was filled with anger, fear, and an overwhelming desire for justice. I, along with Jamie, am all too familiar with the place where, when helplessness sets in, I come to appreciate the feeling of standing on my own two feet, taking charge, and drawing strength from the scars it leaves on those who stand in its way. This is for those of us who are gone, outspoken, and crushed. This serves as a reminder that despite the depths of despair, there was a way out, albeit a tumultuous, disorganised, and agonising one.

Thank you for stepping into this story. I hope it touches you, sparks important conversations, and reassures you that you are not alone.

With gratitude,

Aidan Blackwood

The Escape

The sound of his heartbeat was deafening. Jamie brought his back in contact with the cold brick wall, exhaling in quick, shallow breaths. The smell of damp concrete and stale beer ran thick in the alleyway, and dim light from a streetlight a few blocks away did little to drive out the footsteps descending from the sides.

His fists tightened at his sides, knuckles hurting and throbbing, the pain actually sharp enough to cut through the fog of fear. Somewhere nearby, he could hear them — low voices, laughter that carried a cruel edge. Jamie knew they were looking for him. He hadn't run far enough.

"Little bitch thought he could just walk away," one of them sneered, the words slicing through the night like a blade.

Jamie shut his eyes, continuing to hold himself rigid, to maintain his breathing at a controlled pace. The cold of the pipe echoed in his mind, then the thud of crushing bone, and the burning that had left him sprawled on the ground. He could still smell the blood as bitter and metallic, forming a pool of blood at the back of his mouth.

Don't think about it. **Move**.

But his body refused to listen. His legs felt like lead, his muscles trembling under the weight of the night's events. All he could do was wait — wait and pray that they'd give up, that the echoes of their taunts would fade into the distance.

Instead, their footsteps grew louder, closer.

Jamie made a struggle to exit the alley and into a freezing cold wind. The cold went into his skin; however, it was dwarfed by that of an oppressive weight on top of him. He pulled his hood down and as he went, he kept his head down and made every move further from the alley and closer to Paul's apartment.

The Party

The walk from Alexandria up to Paul's flat in Old Bonhill was brutal: a cold that didn't just nip at you but sank deep into your body. A wind blew straight over the ice-cold waters of the River Leven, howling down the narrow streets, biting with its icy teeth at my exposed skin. A few figures shuffled along the pavement, their heads hunched against the wind, clutching their coats tightly around themselves. Gusts scooped up foul scraps of litter, sending them spiralling off into the darkness. It wasn't a night for lingering outdoors. It was a night that drove houses to shut and people to gather round warm hearth fires, cocooned in throws and hot chocolate to soothe the troubled heart.

The wind was strong, piercing cleanly through my jacket, a chilling reminder of my lack of resistance to the elements. Scotland was accustomed to the cold, but this night sank its teeth deeply into your bones.

Streetlights flickered weakly, their orange halos barely holding back the night while casting long, shivering shadows on the cracked tarmac. The shadows danced with the wind, stretching and warping into grotesque shapes that mocked me as I trudged, their twisted forms seeming to lunge forward, eager to ensnare me in the gloom. My breath fogged in shallow puffs, carried off instantly by the harsh gusts. Desperate to protect myself from the harsh weather, I pulled my hood lower and hunched my shoulders higher, even though it felt like a futile battle.

The closer I came to Paul's place, the more the scheme changed. A solitary shop and lampposts gave way to lines of tired, grey council flats, buildings that sagged under the weight of their own neglect. The paint flaked off in nasty strips, revealing the sun — beaten concrete floor, while boarded-up windows looked like smirking eyes as I walked past. Occasional sounds broke the icy silence: distant voices carrying over the stillness or the faint hum of a car, muffled as though the night swallowed the noise. Far away, unseen, the hoarse barking of a dog resounded, an echo deadened by the heavy, chilled air; what reached my ears almost disappeared. The distant whistling of a train as it crossed over its rails was heard creeping up the silence; the tremor was almost like a spectral whisper of being and moving in a system that appeared otherwise to be static ice.

Not too far away, I began to hear the bassline of music echoing down the street, a muffled beat resonating through the building walls. It wasn't far from Paul's apartment, but it felt as though every step took me deeper into another world. The flat went unnoticed because it was just one of the many identical units lined up in a row. When I reached his door, it stood ajar; light spilt onto the garden steps and out into the path, as did a cacophony of sound: laughter, shouting, the clink of bottles. The music throbbed, the bassline now violently vibrating through the thin walls like the building's pulse.

I stood outside for a moment, listening to the sounds coming from inside — the steady beat of the music and hijinks.

The flat was suffocating from people — one of those parties where the room moved in waves, caught in a shared, chaotic current. The air was dense and hot, thickly imbued

3

with the mingling smells of sweat, smoke, and spilt alcohol. Conversations were indistinguishable, dull tones, punctuated by the odd eruption of laughing. Someone fiddled with the sound system in a corner, sending the music into irregular fits of distortion before it returned to the relentless pounding bass. I weaved through the mass of bodies; I was never confident in social environments, keeping my head low as the music and rising heat pressed in on me, trying to settle my anxiety. It wasn't simple to disappear into the haze of it all. The crowd wasn't interested in me; they were all there to lose themselves, floating away on whatever set of drugs or liquor they could find.

Moving into the kitchen, it was even more packed than the living room, its walls practically sweating from the oppressive heat of all those bodies jammed together. People slouched against the counters, perched on stools, or hovered around the fridge, plastic cups clutched loosely in their hands, as they desperately tried to pour themselves another drink. The table in the centre bore the scars of countless similar nights — its surface scratched, sticky, and buckling under the weight of half empty bottles and makeshift ashtrays. I was handed a cup and as I took a sip; a sharp, burning hit the back of my throat. It was vodka —

pure vodka — now choking on both the vodka and the smoke that lingered in the air.

I weaved towards the back of the room, trying to find a pocket where I could breathe, where the vodka wouldn't feel like it was pounding directly onto my skull. The open window called to me. A couple near the sink argued; their raised voices cut through the music. It was for no obvious reason that they fought, though the air seemed electric with tension between them: he gestured wildly, and she glared, arms crossed tight over her chest.

Those guys, sitting around the table nearby, were laughing too loudly, sloshing alcohol into cups with a reckless abandon that only comes with a certain level of heavy intoxication. One spilt half a bottle across the table; the liquid ran in sticky trails toward the edge, no one making a move to clean it up. They just laughed harder; they slapped each other's back quite forcefully; even he spilt his drink.

The fluorescent light above the table in the kitchen flickered on and off, casting a surreal, strobe like glow that made faces appear disconnected and disjointed. Shadows stretched out and contracted in strange ways, distorting the room's edges and adding to the surreal atmosphere. A hand reached past me and snatched a bottle; they brushed my shoulder before pulling back into the crowd. The crowd pressed in: elbows jabbing my ribs, bodies brushing too close, the odd splash of drink sloshing onto my boots. The walls felt closer, seeming to lean inward, trapping all the noise and heat in one unbearable, inescapable bubble.

Escaping the kitchen and pushing into the living room, Paul was in the corner to the left of the window, precisely where I'd expected him to be. He was sat in a chair that had seen better days, slouched, with one arm draped over the armrest, the other holding a cigarette burning down to the filter. His eyes were half closed; an expression of detached amusement spread on his face as he watched the chaos around him. He caught my gaze with a faint smile, raising his cup in a mock toast and spilling a little of its contents onto the already sticky floor.

"Aye, you made it, man," he mouthed back to me; I could barely make him out over the din. I nodded, not bothering to speak; he wouldn't hear me anyway. The longer I stood there, the more the crowd's energy began to wear me down. The shouting was too sharp, the music too loud, the heat oppressive. The space felt like it was shrinking, the air thick and heavy. I needed to move

I left the living room for the bedroom, but it wasn't much better. The bass line pounded through the floor, causing my heartbeat to become unrhythmic. People swayed in a vague imitation of dancing, most of them dancing too far gone to really be capable of moving with any real coordination. The lights were dimmer in here, casting the room in a murky glow that obscured their faces. That's when I clocked them, a group of five boys standing near the far wall, separated from the rest of the party. They did not join in dancing or drinking; they didn't move with careless abandon like everyone else. They caught my attention, something sharper, harder; I swear I knew them but couldn't quite place them. They stood motionless, their eyes slowly scanning the room with a silent intensity that sent a shiver running down my spine. One of them caught my eye: a tall guy with a shaved head and a messy scar that ran down the side of his cheek, Craig 'Scars' Donnelly, unmistakable with the permanent disfigurement across his cheek and crooked nose, a constant reminder of the violence carved into his skin. His eyes met mine — piercing and precise — and I realised I'd judged this wrong from the start. I should've walked away, kept moving. But something about the way he stared froze me in place, like a predator sizing up its prey.

He leaned forward and whispered back to one of his mates, which he followed up with a nod at me. The friend turned and looked at me, his face impassive but something in his eyes I didn't like. In a few seconds they started to approach me with slow, efficient steps, strolling through the crowd like a blade.

My chest tightened as they closed the distance.

"FUCK," my subconscious urging me to run, to lurk back into the crowd at the party. But it was too late. They were right in front of me, their silhouettes descending over me as a black drape.

"You look lost," Scars is the first to speak, his voice low and rough, laced with menace to make the hair on the back of my neck stand up. Scars company surrounded me, a loose semi-circle of friends forming a blockade with no way out. The crowd around us seemed oblivious, caught up in their own drunken revelry, the music drowning out everything else.

"Fuck off, Scars, I'm just here for a drink," I replied, my voice as evenly tempered as I could get it as I tried to keep my hands from balled fists by my sides.

Scar smirked, his eyes narrowing.

"Aye, is that right? Just here for a drink?" His tone is now mocking; the words are dripping with derision.

"You've got that look about you, as if. you think you are better than us. Like you don't belong here."

I opened my mouth to reply, but before I could, one of his friends shoved me hard in the chest, sending me stumbling back against the wall. Their group erupted in savage, loud laughter. Heat rose in my chest, part anger, part fear.

The edges around the room closing in on me, the crowd thinning, my mind collapsing into a blur. It was just them and me, jeering faces and a razor-sharp line of mockery. I knew with a sickening twisting feeling in the pit of my stomach that this wouldn't end well. Scars' grin widened, creeping, inexorably, as he drew closer — his men trailing behind, a pack of wolves cornering in on their victim. He leaned his head, his eyes gleaming with evil as he appraised me, deriving pleasure from the terror he was causing.

As I squared up to him, I heard him sneer.

"Look who finally emerged from under his rock," his voice a deep, brittle sound like a knife.

"Thought you'd disappeared, mate. What's the matter? Couldn't hack it out there in the real world?" I unclutched my fists as best as I could, holding back my reaction and not satisfying them. However, the words penetrated deeply, piercing the core of everything I'd been attempting to flee.

"Cat got your tongue?" Another piped up, mocking and pleased with himself. He leaned in closer, his breath sour with beer and a hint of something sharper.

"Bet it's because you know what's coming. Don't you?"

"Bet it is, Rydo," Scars cut in, his voice now almost playful, but nothing soft lay in the glint of his eye.

"You've always been simple to read. It reminds me of that night, doesn't it? When you lay there, crying like a wee bitch. Didn't think you'd show your face again after that." My stomach was now filled with anger, yet I remained unmoved. I refused to give them the satisfaction they sought. Then, a skinny, smirking — looking lad chimed in.

"Maybe he likes it, eh? Likes getting put in his place." He reached out, flicking at my jacket dismissively, as if I wasn't even worth his full attention.

"Is that why you came back, then? Want another go?"

Scars laughed, a husky, overbearing sound, which filled the room. Spurring the others to continue

"Reckon, that's it. Knew he couldn't cut it anywhere else. Thought he'd come back; find the old crowd and see if we'd let him in on the fun."

"Not our kind of fun," the wiry one added, his tone singsong and mocking.

"He's too soft for that. Always was. Just another wee pussy playing hardman." Their words had scalded me, each finding its mark with cruel precision. I battled the scalding rage building in my stomach, my fists locking down more and more, nails ripping into my palms.

Scars came closer and closer to the point where I could perceive the sheen of the sweat on his forehead and the crooked forming of the carved scar on the side of his face.

"You've got nothing now, do you?" He purred, a voice low and threatening, just for me.

He was just another piece of crap, wasting space and pretending to be tough, but he remained the same small, sad boy we left bleeding on the ground. His statements tightened around me like a chain, with each sound creating a new link.

I opened my mouth to say something, anything, but before I could, his hand shot out, slamming me hard into the wall. The room tilted: the hum of the party faded in the background as the group closed in, their sniggering sharp and cruel.

"Go on, fucking say something," he jeered, leaning into my face; I could smell a mix of sweat and alcohol clinging to him.

"Say something, and we'll make sure you won't be saying anything for a long while," he sneered. The next shove was more forceful, slamming me against the wall once more, intensifying the force and depriving me of breath. The wiry lanky one came closer, twisting up my arm, the sudden jerk, slammed the pain up my shoulder.

His grin widened when I winced.

"What's the matter? Are you at a loss for words right now? Thought you were the big man." Scars had something in his hand now, turning it over like he was admiring it before passing it to the wiry one. I could tell it was heavy by its dull sound as he handed it over. A pipe or some kind of bar glinted faintly under the flickering light. He held it up, turning it slowly in his hand to let the dim light catch the edges, then pressing it to my chest hard enough. I felt the cold steel biting through my jacket, making me shiver.

"Think he'll remember these scars?" He turned around and looked back at his team with a smirk.

"Reckon, he'll remember the sound it makes. How it'll feel?" The rest laughed, their chorus of evil that reverberated around the room, drowning out the throbbing bass. Scars cocked his head, his grin widening.

"Put on a show for him, Lee; show him who's boss; show him who runs this fucking town."

The first blow came fast; Lee swung the pipe down and struck me square in the stomach. Air went whoosh from my lungs in a sharp, painful. My knees buckled, and I staggered backwards. They didn't stop. Punch, kick, punch, again and again, each one pushing me into the depths of despair until I was tucked in the foetal position on the floor, arms around my head in a vain attempt to shield myself.

"See?" One of them laughed; his cry echoed in my head.

"Just like before. Same little bitch. Same little pussy."

"Except this time," Scars growled; his voice was dark, gleeful.

"He's not getting up." Before I could move, Lee was on my back, his weight crushing me, pinning me down, pressing my face into the rough, grimy floor. Something hard and unyielding pressed against my mouth — the pole's metallic surface biting with brutish precision into my lips and teeth. It ground harder, pressing against my molars and sending a jarring shock through my jaw, as though it might shatter at any second. Panic swelled as I twisted my head, trying to push the pole away with my hands, but the weight from Lee pinned me down completely. I struggled uselessly; every effort of resistance seemed only to drive the cold, relentless pressure deeper, leaving me utterly trapped, powerless beneath them. They were in control, and they made sure I knew it. Scars then gave a sharp, sickening crack and drove his boot into my face. Pain exploded through my jaw, radiating in blinding waves.

The jagged edges of pulled disintegrated teeth ripped at my tongue, and the metallic taste of blood filled my mouth and throat. Lee pulled the bar away, releasing me with a gasp and a choking fit of blood and splinters in my mouth. The sound of their laughter disappeared as they ran off, and only the thump of music and the far, emotionless roar of other voices remained. I was desolate, a limp rag doll, on the floor, unable to move or think at all. My vision dimmed, the edges closing in as the world narrowed to a pulsing, relentless well of pain. I lay down on the floor, curling — God knows how long — minutes, hours, maybe — but suffering floods me in relentless waves. The weight of the pain, humiliation, and isolation descended around me in the form of a suffocating blanket. My mind screaming at me to open my eyes, but even that felt impossible.

The room was empty, its shadows stretching across the walls in strange, jeering shapes. Trembling, I raised my shaking hand; my fingers brushed against my swollen jaw, the sharp edges of teeth broken, and the sticky wetness of blood. Pain was excruciating, an unbearable pulsing ache from which my failure and weakness arose. I tried to raise myself, but my arms shook, and I gave way, reverting me to the floor. All the strength drained from my body. The party had moved on without me; Paul must have assumed I'd left without saying goodbye. Where the fuck had he gone? I must have been out for hours. Scars, Lee, Rydo, and the crew cast me aside like a stray on an empty beach. The music still pulsing faintly in the distance, a hollow, mocking beat that mirrored everything I'd tried and failed to escape. But there was no escape now. There was only darkness, silence, and the sharp, harsh sensation of blood on my taste buds.

I floated about in a fog of concussive pain, struggling to remain awake. A gentle breeze swirled in, bringing with it the musty, rotten smell of the street outside. This reminded me of the life that lurked just beyond the room's threshold — a life that didn't care about what transpired here, what lived here, or what passed along this wall, in this corner, or under this swing.

I was struck by their leering faces, mocking, giggling, and the sickening sound the bar made when it broke my jaw. The sharp, cruel voices reverberated continuously in my mind, with each word piercing deeper into my chest like a knife. The pain dragged me under again, like a riptide, hurtling me into a restless void where the echoes of the night played endlessly, refusing to let me go.

The Meeting

1997, 2 years prior.

The rhythmic clatter of the train wheels along the tracks was constant, near — hypnotic; however, it did little to ease the tight, uneasy knot in the pit of my stomach. Underneath, the grey, even, and unending afternoon sky was a dreich grey oppression that seemed to go on and on, never threatening to be lifted or broken.

The fields and hills smeared in subdued greens and browns sped by as the train made its way along. Bare trees swayed by, branches drawing themselves towards the sky, as did hedgerows, looking like convicts running for their lives from the darkness. I sat by the window, clutching my schoolbag tight to my chest, hands clamped on it as if for protection.

My eyes were fixed on the scuffed-up floor of the carriage, my body pressed into the seat as if I might disappear right into the worn linoleum. But it wasn't working.

Opposite me sat Jason Kerr, slumped with a languid arrogance that had become his trademark. Jason spread his legs wide, occasionally sinking one foot into my shin, a subtle reminder of his presence. Jason was stocky, thickset, and mean in that peculiar, razor-sharp way that only teenage boys could master. It was something he'd honed in the corridors and playgrounds of St. Pat's — his instincts as sharp as a wolf on the hunt. His school uniform was rumpled beyond belief; his white shirt hung loose from his body, and the tie was in a half bow, flapping with every careless movement.

Confidence oozed from him like a musky cologne, honed through years of pushing people around and getting away with it. A shrill, grating laugh cut the air as he jabbed a finger into my chest, leaning forward with a smirk plastered across his face.

"What's up, wee man? Cat got your tongue?" I jerked sideways, my hands instinctively clenching on the straps of my pack.

"I don't want any trouble, Jason." I uttered a rough mutter, my voice shaking slightly. Jason mocked me in an exaggerated, high-pitched whine.

"I don't want any trouble, Jason," he mimicked, his voice thick with scorn.

"What's that, your maw's script for you? Eh? Does she write your wee lines before you leave the house?" Laughter exploded behind him; the usual entourage seated a row back hadn't joined in yet, but their laughter was all the fuel Jason needed to keep going.

My cheeks burnt; the heat crawled up to the tips of my ears. I hated it — the helpless feeling, the humiliation. I despised how the gnawing knot of fear dug its way through my limbs, slowly stealing the fight out of me.

I looked around the carriage desperately for a person to stand up and intercede on my behalf, but the few other passengers stuck their noses into their books or meticulously looked at the countryside racing by, in a manner that was both awkward and clear: nobody was going to intervene. That is, until Jason latched onto the strap of my bag and tugged with all his might, peeling it half off my lap.

"What's in here, eh? Homework? Snacks? Your wee diary, where you write about how much you hate me?"

"Give that back!" I barked, nearly shocked by my own venomous tone.

Jason let his grin widen, and his eyes lit up.

"Oh, we've got some fight in us, have we?" He sneered, wrenching the bag fully from my grasp. I lunged forward, hands scrabbling for the strap. For a brief moment, we engaged in a tense struggle as the bag threatened to swing wildly between us.

Its contents teetered precariously in an eternal balance, ever threatening to spill, as we tussled for mastery over it.

His mates laughed and jeered in delight from their chairs, their loud cackles ringing off the closed carriage walls.

It was sharp, biting the ugliest possible soundtrack to my humiliation.

"Fucking let it go, you little cunt!" Jason snarled, giving the bag one last yank. The force sent me stumbling back into my seat.

Jason was holding the bag aloft like some kind of trophy, rummaging through it one handed and holding it just out of reach with the other.

"What's this?" he sneered, pulling out a battered paperback.

"Some daft book? Bet you think you're clever, don't you?"

"It's mine," I stammered, my voice shaking. "Give it back."

Jason flipped the pages with an intentional disregard for neatness, crumpling corners and smearing the paper with grubby fingers.

"What's this shite, then? Dragons? Wizards? Bet you're one of those fantasy nerds."

"Only give it back," I muttered, my fists clenched deep inside my lap.

He completely ignored me, throwing the book to one of his friends, who caught it laughing and immediately began turning the pages with just as little care. They were passing it back and forth, playing some game, bending the spine so it cracked, pulling at the fragile edges of the pages. My chest tightened in pain, and a caustic mix of anger and humiliation rose to my throat like bile. Finally, Jason heaved the bag back at me. The glaring omission was the book.

"You can keep the rest of your shit," he said, his grin snaking into a smirk as he jerked his chin toward the next stop.

"But don't think that's it. I'll see you in Balloch.". The train screeched to a stop, the screeching brakes splitting the quiet as it rolled into the station. Jason shoved his hands deep inside his jacket pockets, adopting an arrogant swagger toward the doors, his smirk fixed on his face. His mates trailed behind, throwing backward glances in my direction with amusement and expectation etched across their faces.

I sat still, my heart pounding, my hands trembling as I pushed everything else in my bag aside. My eyes flicked nervously around the other passengers. They all kept their noses buried in books and newspapers, oblivious or so pretending to be. One pair of eyes flowed my way: a boy behind a few rows, his long legs sprawled lazily across the aisle. Older, probably sixteen or seventeen, he wore his hood up over dark cropped hair, and sharp angular features masked an expression — one of relaxed coolness and detachment — that read as if he saw all without giving anything in return. Neither moved nor said a word, yet his eyes stayed fixed on me, unblinking, weighing me up in some balance of judgement.

The doors of the train hissed open. Despite having lead legs, I managed to pull myself up. There was just no way I couldn't do what had to be done; it was quite literally no choice at all for me to stay inside the train. Jason was already on the platform, leaning against a metal beam and folding his arms across his chest, the smug grin still plastered on his face.

His crew stood together, their stances casual yet charged, as if they were anticipating the arrival of World Wrestling Entertainment or a similar spectacle. I stepped off the train, my stomach twisting in on itself, and headed for the stairs over to the overpass. There was the faint scuff of footsteps behind me. I turned back, caught a glimpse of the boy from the train, his hood still up, following just far enough back that no one else would notice. Jason hadn't marked him yet.

I climbed the first flight, rough concrete scraping against my soles with every step. Every onwards step wiped it out; as a matter of fact, there was only the narrow overhead pass or the rather ambitious scheme of Levenvale facing forward, stretching across to span towards the opposite side of the road.

Jason's footsteps drew nearer, becoming more audible with each heartbeat. It grew louder, the sound of Jason's feet with each second closing in. Up the stairs to the left at the top, onto unsteady ground, and steps that carried me up to the crossing, the wind howled through gaps in the metal railings, and its sharp, stinging chill bit my cheeks. The wind carried Jason's low, taunting voice for me to hear before I heard the sound of his feet.

"You can't run forever, mate!" Jason sneered; his laughter carried across the empty expanse of the sparsely landscaped ground with a narrow path. A different sound sliced through his laughter; footsteps, heavier and surer footed, bounced off the concrete. Jason's words choked mid taunt; his tone turned to puzzlement.

"Who the fuck are you?" I didn't turn back; I didn't need to.

I knew the hooded boy wasn't far behind. For the first time that day, a glimmer of hope broke through the tension constricting my chest. Jason spun around, his trademark swagger slipping the instant his eyes landed on the hooded boy. The hooded boy was closer now, not having creaked a single shoe, hands in his jacket pockets, his gait loose, and somehow deliberate.

His demand for attention manifested itself in the form of even steps, a firm outline around his jawline, and calm eyes that did not flutter. Jason's frown deepened, and for the first time, his veneer of confidence cracked.

"What's your problem, mate?" Jason said gruffly, his voice breaking between anger and embarrassment.

The hooded boy didn't say anything right away. He stopped behind Jason a few steps, his head cocked in such a way as to regard him with detached curiosity. For a moment, the quiet between them pulled taut, almost crackling with unsaid tension.

"You like picking on folk who can't fight back?" he asked finally, his voice low and direct, sharp enough to cut through the cold wind. Jason huffed loudly, a high pitched, derisive snort that was sharp and meant to intimidate. What's it to you? That little prick's not your concern. He took one step closer — the hooded boy, his hands deep into jacket pockets, his posture relaxed, unmoved.

"I hate bullies," he said, firm and chilly, and his voice sliced into the tension filled air. Jason puffed himself out, his shoulders going rigid as he tried reclaiming that dominant position of his.

"Aye? And what're you gonna do about it, tough guy?" He jabbed his finger into the boy's chest, but it was a very juvenile manner; the gesture was hollow and weak in its attempt at intimidation. In an instant, the boy snatched his wrist, twisting it sharply, hauling him off balance before Jason could even blink. As Jason fell forward, the boy reached in and smashed his forehead into Jason's face with a harsh, sickening crack.

The force of the headbutt resonated in the silent air with chilling precision. Jason reeled backward, clutching at his nose, blood gushing between his fingers while tears streamed down his face. His mates stood frozen, their eyes wide with disbelieving glances. None of them dared go a step farther.

"You broke my nose, ya fuckin' psycho!" Jason screamed out, his voice thick and muffled, warped by the pain.

The hooded boy remained unfazed. He reached out with one of his hands; he extended his reach, and as the intervening distance closed with a glacial calm, his gaze weighed down Jason.

"Next time you want to start something," The boy spoke in a low, even voice, infusing every word with threat.

"Make sure you can finish it." Jason didn't say anything. Jason focused on halting the blood flow, his confidence in ruins. Jason's friends came to life, one reaching for each arm as they pulled him down the steps toward the stairs that would lead back to the silent train. None of them once looked around in their panic. The youth with the hood stayed there, unmoved, watching them leave, as his face said nothing that could be read into it, then turned to me. I stood fixed at the top of the stairs, my breath caught between overwhelming relief and unbelief.

"You all right?" he asked, his voice removed as he climbed the last few steps to me.

I nodded, my voice faltering, finally coming out.

"Y...yeah... thanks," I croaked; the words seemed so futile.

The boy shrugged slightly, sliding his hands back into his pockets.

"Don't mention it," he replied simply.

His eyes ran down the stretch of road where Jason and his crew had vanished from sight, and for a second, his visage darkened.

"Idiots like them never learn," he said quietly, his tone cold with conviction.

"Unless somebody teaches them a proper lesson." I scrutinised him intently, unsure whether I should utter a single word. There was something about him: smaller than his apparent age, yet in so many ways far older. It was not

just the sharp features but the way he carried himself —
one who had seen too much and learnt to endure.

"You're at school, aye?" He ventured lightly, tone
piercing the silence.

"Third year, St. Pat's." I said, he nodded once in
acknowledgement, probably filing the answer away in
whatever mental notebook he kept.

"I was at Vale Academy. Didn't hang around long,
though." I had no idea if that meant he had dropped out
early or had merely moved along, and I didn't ask. In his
tone of voice lay a guardedness, some quiet wall that
indicated a preference that certain subjects were simply
best not touched on.

"You catch this train every day?" he asks, his sharp eyes
cutting back to mine again.

"Most days," I said, and suddenly felt naked, exposed to
his keen and steady regard.

"That is the only way to school from here." He nodded
again. The edge he had held to in both voice and eyes
gentled off a notch.

"I'm Paul, by the way. Stay close next time.".

"People like him, talk's all they've got. But they hate
losing face. Might try something stupid later." The thought

sent a shiver coursing through me, but something in Paul's calm certainty kept me anchored.

"Why'd you help me?" I blurted, the question slipping out before I could stop it. Paul cocked his head to one side, a faint, flickering smile tugging the corner of his mouth. Like I said, I hate bullies, he said matter of factly, as if it were some kind of essential fact about himself. There was nothing arrogant in his tone, no haughtiness, just a low, quiet certainty that dared argument.

"Thanks, I'm Jamie," I said, this time with feeling. Paul nodded and set off in the general direction of Levenvale, loose limbed, in no hurry as if he'd got all the time in the world. There had been a weight in the air just that second before, a tightness that pressed on the lungs; now it wasn't. Now it was lighter, easier to breathe. A few steps on, he turned back, facing me.

"You heading home?" Paul asked,

"Aye Paul," I was now running to close the distance between us. We walked together down that deserted road, the icy wind whipping against our faces. Surprisingly enough, the silence that fell between us was easy, and for the first time in what felt like forever, I didn't feel alone. This was the beginning of something that I might never, perhaps ever, understand until much later.

Paul had the ability to infiltrate your life, then surge in with a ferocious intensity. Over time, he emerged as a rare individual I could rely on: a person who would not remain silent when faced with challenges. He was a man perfectly acquainted with darkness — the kind of lad who had learnt not only to survive it but also to step through it with unflinching eyes. And in that instant, trudging along the cold, desolate road by his side, I felt for the first time that maybe — just maybe — I wasn't lost after all.

Aftermath

The thing I was first to notice was light. Blind, antiseptic, and cold, it forced itself against my sealed eyelids with a persistent pressure that drove the beating in my skull to the next level. It wasn't warm or cosy; it cut through the mental haze like a fucking knife.

Upon opening my eyes, the world appeared fragmented, shimmering and blurring through the lens of smudged glass. For a moment, I floated in disorientation, untethered, with no sense of where I was or how I'd gotten here.

My surroundings were a tangle of unfamiliar shapes, shadows blending into sharp edges, reality refusing to solidify. Then the pain hit. It emanated from each and every part of my body in a visceral, churning tide, immense and unyielding. With each deep breath, stones ground against my chest, and the marks of bruising and cuts across my body were living testaments of a body overloaded beyond its capacity.

It was inescapable, impossible to disentangle one source of suffering from another. The rhythm was unending and total, leaving me with a sensation of pulverisation into nothingness. My jaw screamed in protest with every shallow inhale. Something was terribly wrong.

A tightness clamped my face in a way that shouldn't have been there. That is, when I attempted to shift, a new stabbing of pain shot past my focus, white hot and sharp. Instinctively, I raised a shaking hand to my chin. What I felt wasn't entirely flesh. Beneath the overfilled skin, my fingertips tapped onto cold, rigid metal. A web of wires, tightly woven around my jaw, locked it in place, forcing my teeth together in an iron grip. A chill swept through me as panic surged.

My mouth. My jaw.

It was wired shut. The realisation gnawed at me, causing me to instinctively leap out of bed and scramble to open my mouth. Every contracting of muscle caused a new wave of pain shooting all the way through my head and down my neck like fire and ice. I collapsed back onto the bed, trembling, my breath coming in ragged gasps through my nose. Trapped. Helpless. The wires locked my words inside me, stealing the only weapon I could use for now to fight back.

A wave of claustrophobic despair washed over me, heavy and suffocating, as I struggled to accept that this was real. The memories came in jagged flashes, broken shards of a night I couldn't fully piece together. The scent of stale beer and cigarettes filled the air. The menacing bassline of the music pulsates through the room. A dense fog of smoke enveloped the room as their bodies pressed together, radiating heat. Then their faces. Older. Harder. Five of them. And him. Craig 'Scars' Donnelly. The scar on his face was a manifestation of brutality, etched as a narrative across his body. His gaze was as icy and calculating as his actions that night.

He'd looked at me with the kind of amusement reserved for a bug squirming underfoot. I remembered the others flanking him, jeering, circling like predators closing in. And then there was the bar. The memory of Lee jamming the cold metal between my teeth came rushing back with brutal clarity. I could still hear it the sickening crunch as my jaw shattered, the metallic taste of blood flooding my mouth.

Their roar was a deafening echo as I collapsed motionless to the ground, unable to do anything, lost in agony. The memory burnt like acid, twisting in my gut, fanning the flames of something darker inside me. Now I was here, on a hospital bed under the fluorescent lights, looking at rows of sterile machines that pulsed and droned in mechanical impassiveness. The room was too bright, too clean, a stark contrast to the chaos in my head. And here I was pale, swollen, and broken. The nurse appeared at last, efficient and brisk in her motions. She maintained a detached expression. She checked the machines and adjusted the IV, her practiced hands moving with the ease of someone who had seen it all before.

"You've got multiple fractures in your jaw," she said, her voice calm and clinical.

"The doctors wired it shut to help it heal. It's going to take time, but you'll recover." She continued. She continued, treating this as if it were a minor scratch that needed no further attention. I tried to meet her gaze — to make her understand the pain, the anger, and the humiliation I couldn't put into words. But she gave me only a polite, hollow smile, her attention already shifting to the next task.

"You'll be on a liquid diet for the next couple of months," she said, almost casually.

There were weeks filled with indifference and mediocrity. I spent weeks in silence. I spent weeks trapped inside my own head. It wasn't recovery. It was a fucking prison sentence. She left me on my own, the oppressive quiet heightened by the soft click of the door. Every forced sip of the thick, bland shakes they brought me was a bitter reminder of what I'd lost. Each silent husk fuelled the simmering fire in my heart. By the fourth day, I'd settled into the monotony of my new existence.

The nurses moved in and out, their faces merging into one, their words meaningless as they blended with the steady breath of machines. The bruises on my skin began to fade, shifting into sickly shades of yellow and green, but the pain in my jaw remained constant, a relentless reminder of my helplessness. Then, a knock broke the quiet.

It wasn't a nurse or a doctor who stepped into the room. It was a man. He stood in the doorway with all of his physical bulk, weathered and angular, his face a mask of impassiveness. He had crumpled his suit and slicked back his grey hair, adding a small touch of control to his otherwise dishevelled appearance.

"Detective Fraser," he announced, dragging a chair against the side of the bed. He crawled down into it with a flourish and looked at me with an expressionless gaze that betrayed more horrors than he could possibly have seen.

"I heard you had a rough night." His voice was calm and measured, but there was an edge to it, a weight that made it clear he wasn't here to offer sympathy. I gazed at him, my silence amplifying his words. Fraser leaned forward, his voice dropping a fraction.

"Do you think they're done with you? Do you think this ends here?" I didn't need him to tell me what I already knew. This wasn't over. It was just the beginning. He studied me for a long moment, his sharp gaze probing, as though trying to pry loose a reaction. Unsurprised at my silence, or at least the lack of response, he sucked in a deep breath and leaned back in his own chair, bringing his arms across his chest.

"You're young," he said, his tone steady, deliberate.

"You've got your whole life ahead of you. But I've seen kids like you before, lying in hospital beds just like this. Refusing to talk. Thinking they can handle it on their own." His words hung in the air like smoke, curling into the cracks of my thoughts. He wasn't wrong. I firmly believed within myself that I could handle this situation independently, without the need for others to contribute to my solution. But hearing him say it out loud with that edge of weary authority made it feel heavier.

"There are people who can assist," Fraser murmured, his voice echoing with a different effect — a softer rather than an imperative tone, a worn-out tone.

"But you've got to let them help." I looked out the window at the distance, the world seemingly out of reach. Cars went about their business in slow, robotic, marching motions across the street below. People bustled on the pavement, their lives untouched by what had happened to me. I wanted to be out there. Moving. Free from this room and its oppressive walls. But Fraser wasn't going to let me drift.

"You know they won't give up on you?" he probed.

"Because they won't. They'll come back. Maybe not tomorrow, maybe not next week. But they'll find you. And when they do," I cut him short with a stare that would make a shark stop in its tracks and my jaw throb from the exertion. I didn't need him to finish the sentence. I'd been thinking it ever since I woke up in this bed. They weren't through with me yet. It was far from over. Fraser must have seen the anger in my eyes because he nodded, leaning in again.

"Do something about it," he said, his voice husky and forcing.

"But do it smart. Don't make it worse by playing the lone wolf. By retaliating," he knew it would be futile, but he was determined not to give up. His lecture hung in the air; he admitted defeat for now. I wasn't for talking, and with a long sigh, slapping his hands on his thighs, he was on his feet, making his way for the door — the quiet squeak of the door sealing them shut. Alone again, I lay in bed staring at the ceiling, but inside, a storm had begun to stir. Days blurred, a succession of dull pain and simmering anger. The nurses, in dreary tans, went about their motions with a robotic efficiency. Their faces blurred into a faceless sea; their voices reduced to background noise against the steady pulse of the machines. The protein shake they brought me tasted worse with each passing day, thick and tasteless, sticking to the back of my throat like regret.

I tracked the flow of time by the amount of light that streamed in the window. The pale grey of dawn melted into the sterile white of midday, which faded into the oppressive blue of night. Outside, the world moved on without me, uncaring. I hated it for that. Fraser's words circled back to me more often than I wanted. They reverberated in my brain, accusing me of their validity. He was right. They wouldn't stop. They would come for me again. But even if they did, I would not be the same person they'd left broken and lying in the bedroom that night.

Something had to change. I had to change. The wires weren't out yet, and I was still in that bed, with the constant drone of machines and the sterile, cold routine of the hospital room serving as a backdrop. But something inside me had already shifted. The desolateness that had gripped me during the first days, dense as a tomb, had vanished.

Something harsher, colder, and sharper had risen and replaced it: a burning, unspoken commitment. I experienced it each time I looked at the ceiling. Each time I swallowed one of those tasteless shakes they delivered, I just glimpsed my image in the glass of the window. A fog enveloped me, leaving me lost in an unsolvable wasteland between dreaming and waking. The gentle, pulsating sound of the machines that strapped me down held me prisoner in my disorientation. It was quiet, almost peaceful, until the door creaked open.

This wasn't the nurse with her practiced, stealthy tread. This was different. Heavier. Deliberate. Every step echoed through the air, cutting through the surrounding smoke.

The sound dragged at my consciousness, forcing me upward from the numb stupor I'd been floating in. I forced my eyes open. Every blink was a half arse attempt, and my head was throbbing, wincing from the bright fluorescent light coming in from the hallway.

Visitors

Across the blur, a stocky shape came into view and blocked out the light. Mick 'The Boss' McAllister stood in the doorway, filling it with his presence. His dark coat was tailored to the highest standard, and his silver hair was combed back with the precision of a man who understood his own strength and wielded it at will.

Mick exuded an aura of restrained authority, a quiet, commanding power that earned respect without needing to request it. To most, he was a successful businessman, if one could call it that. His empire flourished in the dark, under cover of respectability. But to me, Mick was something else. He was my mentor, the only guiding influence I'd had in this harsh world. He had welcomed me, guided me through the challenges, and, in the process, firmly established me in his life. His life inextricably entwined devotion and loyalty, making it impossible to escape.

As he stepped further into the room, his eyes settled on me, steady and surveying, as though even now he was weighing my worth. I wanted to prove I was strong, unbent. However, even the slightest movement brought a sharp, stabbing ache in my jaw. My face throbbed, a relentless reminder of my helplessness. The wires binding my jaw mocked me, a cruel symbol of just how much I'd lost.

He then sat down in the chair next to my bed and crossed one leg over the other. Coolly impenetrable, Mick dominated the space without a word, his unspoken presence settling heavily upon me. His eyes lingered on the bruises and swollen tissues of my face, and a barely perceptible smirk formed at the corners of his mouth.

"Heard you got yourself into a bit of trouble," he said, his tone holding something I couldn't quite place: humour, pity, or maybe pride.

He eyed me with an expression that was equal parts acknowledgement and judgment. He knew exactly what had gone down. He found it almost amusing, as though this was a predestined event for me.

"They got you good, didn't they?" he asked, as if we were discussing nothing more serious than a scraped knee.

Anger bubbled inside me, a red hot surge of frustration. I was filled with frustration towards him, towards them, and towards myself for allowing it to occur. However, I pretended to make a rigid nod, with each movement inflicting a new wave of pain into my face. He observed me intently, and his fingers tapped a slow measure on the armrest, his black eyes shining with a gentle but powerful intensity. It's true, he started, and the scowl returned to his voice,

"Most of them would have quit years ago. After something like this, they'd be long gone, looking for a clean slate far, far away from here. But you…"

He trailed off, narrowing his eyes as if he saw something in me worth keeping.

"You're still here," he continued, his voice quieter now.

"That tells me you're not like them." His words washed over me, mingling with the resentment, the pain, and the odd sense of validation that his approval seemed to bring.

Mick's admiration was something to be cherished, and despite the circumstances, that part of me still held close to me with the glue of a balm over my bare, stripped core. He leaned in and, in a hushed, almost confessional way, he lowered his voice.

"I know who did this to you. Rest assured, they will face the consequences. But revenge," his eyes locked onto mine, steady and unyielding, communicating something wordless yet understood.

"Revenge is a slow game."

Mick never acted impulsively. He never struck without calculating every move. He thrived on precision and patience and expected the same from me. He saw vengeance not as a reaction, but as a process that required meticulous precision. I'd have to wait. I'd have to trust him. But deep inside, something rebelled against this restraint, rejecting his terms. To Mick, this was just business, another line on his ledger of debts that he would soon call to be settled and on his terms. But to me, it was personal. To imagine writing, to let him manipulate this aspect of my pain, was bile — making and infuriating. I tried to respond, to tell him I wanted them to suffer as I had, to feel the bone crushing helplessness they'd inflicted on me. However, wires chewed my speech into harsh, frustrated noises.

Mick heard the anger, though. He understood it. He firmly grasped my shoulder, reassuring me. His face was the same grim combination of pity and price calculation.

"Lad," he mumbled, his voice softer but no less earnest,

"There will be plenty of time for that. For now, work on getting stronger. When the time comes, you'll want to be ready." His eyes bored into mine, unblinking, like a silent vow that I would have my chance but only when he decided the time was right.

There was no questioning in his tone, no room for disagreement. Mick's hand squeezed my shoulder in final reassurance or maybe a reminder of who held the reins.

"Good!" he said, straightening as he stood.

"I knew you'd understand." He fastened his coat, looking at me for a final second.

"Rest up, lad. You're going to need all the strength you can get where you're going." And with that, he vanished. His footsteps ran down the hallway, and the room got distinctly colder and quieter. The antiseptic quiet pressed down on me again, heavy and suffocating. I lay there staring at the ceiling, my thoughts churning, anger swirling inside me with no outlet.

Days blurred together in that small, impersonal room. The nurses came and went, their hands moving in silent routine, their eyes flickering with polite detachment as they adjusted IVs and checked monitors. For them, I was just another patient, another mutilated face in their endless series of injuries and suffering. They brought me smoothies and protein shakes — anything liquid and flavourless, I could sip through a straw. Each sip was a bitter reminder of how powerless I'd become. I hated every humiliating moment.

The quiet glances. The clinical touches left a lasting impression. The slimy, flavourless goo mocks me with every sip. It wasn't just the food; it was the whole experience. Everything seemed diminished, as if they had stripped me of my humanity and reduced me to a mere broken body. Every night, as the ward grew quiet, my rage flared up, filling the void and nearly crushing my soul. The memory of that night replayed relentlessly in my head; every detail burned into my mind. I could still taste the metallic taste of blood, feel the snap of bone, and feel the searing agony. I'd lie there in the dark, staring up at the ceiling, my nerves still screaming with the echoes of that night.

What was even worse than the pain, as well as the memories, was the silence. The silence was the true torture. Being confined to my own mind, unable to speak, unable to release the rage clawing at me from the inside, it felt like being buried alive. I had never experienced such suffocating helplessness, such a complete inability to fight back. My anger built with every thought, every memory, twisting my pain into something darker and sharper.

I didn't just want justice. I wanted them to suffer. I wanted them to experience what I experienced: the paralysis, the terror, the crippling pain of being shattered. I wanted to regain control over what they'd stolen, to rebuild each and every bit of myself they'd broken. And yet, even as that storm churned inside me, Mick's words lingered like a quiet warning.

"Revenge is a slow game." I hated that he was right. I detested the connection between my desire for vengeance and his plans. My pain, my anger — they'd become assets in Mick's arsenal, tools he would wield when the time was right.

The idea punched a hole in me as a bitter little pill I had no choice but to take. I needed him. I needed his power, his resources, and his knowledge. So, I waited. Day after day, I lay there in that cold hospital bed, sipping tasteless shakes and letting the anger build. I became something else — a vessel for vengeance. Every fibre of me focused on the promise of retribution. The sensation of cold metal against my teeth, the click of bone, and the burning pain intensified. They played on a relentless loop in my mind, and there was no escaping them.

The images weren't just reminders; they were fuel, stoking the fire inside me. And with every viewing, the fury fermented, transforming into resolution. But purpose alone wasn't enough to quell the frustration. I found myself in a state of impasse, unable to act or release, while the avalanche continued to accumulate within my body. Every moment of silence, every bland sip, and every clinical caress seemed to be a burden of bricks pushing down upon me and holding me captive.

The nurses didn't notice. To them, I was just another patient, a case to manage, a body to heal. They went about their established patterns with mechanical ease, their hands fiddling with IVs and taking notes when the detached way they did it all the time indicated. Whenever they offered me another smoothie or protein shake, I could scream. But I couldn't. The helplessness buzzed in my jaw, a dull beat, unyielding in its insistence on bringing me back to the brink of my utter disintegration. The days dragged on, each one indistinguishable from the next, and the anger inside me solidified. It turned darker, more inescapable, a power that subsumed all of me. I hated the silence. I hated the nurses and their detached stares.

I lost appetite for that slimy, flavourless goo they made me take. However, best of all, I despised myself for being here, for being pathetic, and for submissively allowing them to inflict it on me. Still, in the midst of that bile, Mick's voice filled my thoughts.

"Rest up, lad. You're going to need all the strength you can get." His vow of retribution, out there in the ether, was like a rope dragging me away from the abyss of despair.

I hung on to it not in the desire but in the necessity. Mick was my only way out of this. He was the only one that could set me right. And so, I waited for the moment when Mick would finally give the word. When that moment arrived, I would not hesitate. I would be ready.

And they would pay for everything.

The bruises on my face were fading now, their hues shifting to sickly yellows and greens. The jagged scar along my chin was getting better, but it didn't help any. I no longer experience the reflex flinch when the nurses wistfully looked down at me, their gazes a medley of empathy with clinical nonchalance.

I didn't mind their gossip or their sneaky stares. Let them stare. Let them wonder. Every day I spent in this bed only rekindled the flame within me. I no longer felt broken. The routine around me stayed the same. Nurses arrived and departed, their features one in the same, and their voices a dull drone far away under the constant beat of the machines.

Time went by in odd, broken fragments: the changing light through the window, the detached sounds down the hall. None of it mattered. My focus was elsewhere. Fraser's words kept resonating in my mind, the pressure of their weight bearing down on me.

"Do you think they'll just leave you alone now..." He was right. They weren't done with me. If they weren't done, then they would not be coming for the same person they left behind. I couldn't afford to be.

Leaving the Hospital

A good few weeks after they'd wired my jaw shut, they were finally letting me out. They handed me a prescription for painkillers and a stiff smile, the entire process impersonal and efficient. I pondered whether they recognised my name or if I was just another young man struggling with the life he had unintentionally entered. For them, I was a warning, a testimony to the fact that things could quite easily take a disastrous turn.

Another nurse offered something rehearsed in the way of a 'sympathetic' look as she handed me my discharge papers, reserved only for those to whom she hoped to see again next week. I wanted to laugh, confess to her that I was unique, and say that I wasn't coming back. Wires in my jaw held my words captive, making any utterance I made turn into some low grunt that made her glance off and uncomfortable. On the street, the air was harsh, and standing for a second, I simply exhaled it, the sting of it against my skin. The world seemed sharper somehow, everything more vivid than I remembered, from the dull green trees by the car park to the chipped red paint on the hospital doors.

Weeks and weeks shut up in that sterile, whitewashed room had almost made me forget what it was like to feel the grit of the world on my skin. Sitting on the curb with the engine running steadily was a recognisable car. I turned and saw Paul in the driver's seat, his fingers tapping on the wheel. He nodded, eyes flicking over my bruised face, into an expression that held equal parts of sympathy and wry amusement. Paul had been with Mick for years, a quiet, reliable figure who knew these streets like his own skin. He was the kind that you wouldn't see until he decided it was time you should see him.

"Rough go, eh?" He said jokingly as I settled into the passenger seat, wincing as pain shot through my jaw. I only nodded; fists clenched tight in my lap. Paul accelerated, shifting gears, pulling away from the curb, and focussing on the road. The silence was thick, filled with unspoken words. We took a drive through Alexandria with the grey skies overhead, the streets familiar images whizzing by all around us. Literally, all looked quite the same way, but I was undergoing a different experience, as if everything I was looking at was something new. Every crack in the pavement and every dilapidated building was a reminder of the world I'd chosen — the world that had almost destroyed me. An hour and a half later we stopped at a row of unassuming block flats in the outer part of the scheme. I knew it was one of Mick's "safe spots" — a place to go if I needed to disappear. It was a quiet, out of the way place where nobody would ask any questions. Paul turned over a key, his face impassive.

"Mick's orders," he reminded me. He wants you to stay here, keep reorganising, and grow stronger before he brings you back into the fold. This approach will lead to fewer questions.

I grabbed the key, and nodding, I moved towards the door. The flat was chilly and dark, with a stale smell permeating the empty rooms. It felt like a cell, and that seemed intentional. Mick wanted me alone, focused, with no distractions. The habit now made me scrutinise every room that I passed through in the apartment, looking at myself in the mirror near the door. I was ghostly pale, bruised, and hollow eyed. The swelling had subsided, but the cuts and bruises lingered, darkening my skin with shades of purple and yellow. The gloomy room light reflected the tightly wired jaw. It served as a stark reminder of all the harm they had inflicted upon me. I turned away, not wanting to see the person staring back. I didn't recognise him. Fragility was a luxury I could not afford, leaving me bruised and broken.

The days fell into a grim routine. Mick's contacts visited regularly, providing food, provisions, or anything I wanted. Every visit was a reminder that he hadn't forgotten me, but it felt like I was being watched to see if I was following his plan. Paul dropped by every few days, always bringing bags of protein shakes and soft food that didn't require chewing. Every tasteless swallow was another reason for me to remember how useless I had become, a fact that, now, worked on my temper as I was forcing the concoction down. On the third day Paul came into the room with a gym bag and dropped it unceremoniously to the floor with a soft thump that rang out over the quiet room.

"Mick suggested you might like to begin training," he replied, pointing at the bag.

"Weights and gloves are essential tools to assist you in getting back on your feet." Inside were hand weights, boxing gloves, and resistance bands. It wasn't much, but it was a start. Just as I became aware of the equipment, a fresh determination surged through me. Mick wasn't offering a road to recovery so much as giving me a weapon. Each lift, each punch, each exercise was a step toward becoming the person I needed to be. I forced myself out of bed in the mornings, teeth clenched against the ache in my jaw as I wrapped my hands and fastened the gloves. The first time my fist struck the bag, pain shot through me, yet I didn't stop. I let the pain fuel me, every punch a reminder of what they'd done.

Despite the weights feeling heavier than they appeared and my arms trembling from the strain, I persevered, navigating the delicate balance between fatigue and exhaustion. My muscles screamed in pain, but I welcomed the pain — pain that blotted out the fury simmering inside, a fury poised to break free. Punches are sharper; weights are lighter. More important, it was a mental shift. Every exercise was a taking back of my agency, a confirmation that I was not powerless, that I could still resist. After my set one afternoon, the knock at the door happened. I opened the door and saw Mick standing there, his face unreadable in relation to my sweat — soaked, breathless appearance.

"Looking stronger," he said, and he stepped inside.

"Good. You'll need it." He reclined on the arm of the couch, palms up.

"I stopped in to do a progress check and chat about what's coming up next." I nodded, finding it difficult to speak over the wires, but Mick saw me, his gaze unwavering.

"They'll pay," he said, his every word calculated.

However, the execution must be precise. No, nobody can just charge in swinging their fists; it will burn us all."

"You understand?" I nodded, although each instinct told me to ignore him, to inflict upon them the same pain as I was enduring myself.

But Mick's eyes had a warning in them, a reminder my rage wasn't enough. This was his world, and if I was going to stay alive, I would have to follow his rules. He leaned in, voice low.

"We've got jobs lined up," pausing for a moment

"It involves observing the shipment and ensuring they arrive at their intended destination." I went to reply, and he cut me off.

"Just the beginning. You'll be earning, working your way back." It wasn't what I wanted to do, but I felt I had no choice; I nodded.

Mick was laying out a way forward for me, which implicitly pledged I'd get my recompense one day. He clamped a hand on my shoulder, firm.

"You're one of us now. This life, this pain — it's yours. You learn to carry it, or it'll break you." His words were direct: I had to sleep, eat, and strengthen my body. Each step, each gym routine, each moment, brought me back to the pain I endured, closer to the revenge I so craved. I didn't just want to recover; I wanted to be unbreakable. Mick's team followed me, their times of appearance as routine and fixed as that of a clock. Someone would depart with a car full of supplies and remain absent for several months.

It felt less and less like support and more like surveillance. Mick's daily routine was characterised by a blend of respect and fear, and he consistently instilled in me the expectation to conform and fulfil my responsibilities. It felt like a strange boot camp in a terrible beginning where each day was a challenge. My hands felt like part of the boxing gloves; the weights felt right in my hands, and pain, the thing I had once been so afraid of, had turned out to be a friend.

I just wanted to show myself that it wasn't that broken kid I saw in the mirror — that with each ounce of suffering, I was making something stronger, something invincible. That morning Paul arrived with a duffle bag, heavier than usual.

"Get dressed," he said in the same flat voice but with an edge of seriousness; it was new to me.

He gave me that nod, one that said, It's time. I put on a worn old jacket; the stiff leather felt uncomfortable against my body, and I stepped out of the flat and into the car with him. We sat in silence on the narrow, twisting lanes of Alexandria, rain falling sideways, blurring the edges of the small town into hazy grey shapes. The familiar seemed altered, as if reality had shifted during my absence in the hospital, and I was adjusting my senses.

The car pulled up in front of a small, dilapidated warehouse on the outskirts of Bonhill; its windows were darkened, and a faded sign hung above it. Paul gestured for me to get out; his face was unreadable, and I followed him through the rusted side door. Inside, Mick was sitting, reclined against a stack of boxes, languid in pose but with eyes vigilant and watchful appraisal. He looked at me over the rough surface of the concrete floor, the screen lighting up my entire body at the radius of one glance.

"So," he said in a low, measured tone,

"I hear you're coming along." I made a nod, and my whole body went stiff with eagerness; every fibre was tense and coiled, but he held up a hand.

"Good. You're going to need it." He swivelled, pointing to the other end of the room where two guys were leaning against the wall with an expression of indifference but waiting with childlike enthusiasm. They'll get you back on your feet properly. A little test to see if you can handle yourself in the real world again. The guys straightened and moved toward me, with their eyes glittering with curiosity and reasoning.

Adrenaline surged; I tensed and braced myself, my muscles brought up to full coiling. The blow struck swiftly, striking the ribcage in a straight line, but I managed to dodge it by slipping and ducking low. The thrill of motion — the thrill of every muscle knowing how to do what it was trained to do so powerfully — was muted as I grabbed one of the hurtling blows.

We made a bitter, savage dance of blows and evaded blows; each blow my hands connected with a drumming into flesh, my feet unconsciously dancing to the beat.

Every strike and every grunt felt like life was rebuilding itself again, reminding me of what I'd been working towards.

The second swung at my jaw, and for one moment, I felt that spike of pain I so knew, but I pushed through it, twisting out of reach, my fist landing square against his side. Eventually, I was panting, my chest heaving, with both men backing off, eyeing me with respect if not a touch of wariness. Mick made a very discreet nod, and as I saw it, for the first time a nearly unnoticeable smile passed his lips.

"Not bad," he said.

"Now, we've got some work to do. We're starting with minor tasks, not requiring any heroic efforts. We're talking shipments, keeping tabs, and making sure things run smoothly." He paused, letting his words sink in.

"You follow orders, you prove yourself, and soon enough… there'll be other opportunities." I met his gaze and knew this was his way of offering me a route to the revenge I wanted.

It wasn't the wild, reckless payback I'd once imagined, but something controlled and precise, a means to get my hands dirty, to prove myself on his terms. Every strike, every drop of blood, and every inch of toil was a step closer to tomorrow that I could no longer ignore. Pain and rage have all helped the scheme. Mick's world had shown me its darkness, and I wanted to conquer it. One day, once I was ready, I would demonstrate my abilities to them.

The Point of No Return

Time gradually drew closer to itself, with each day smoothly transitioning into the next, consistent and relentless, akin to the excruciatingly slow trickle of a dripping tap in the darkness. My life was a blur of fists and sweat, an endless cycle of exertion and exhaustion. I hid my face, swallowing everything that Mick threw at me. With every challenge, the weight became greater and greater until it tested the limits of my endurance. Now there was a rhythm — a dark beat of work, training, and recovery.

My days and nights had merged into a harsh symphony of motion and silence. Each bead of sweat that trickled from my forehead to the ground made me realise that Mick was not only trying to coach me; he was trying to prepare me. He was pushing me towards the brink of my potential. Daring me to snap or shatter. But I wouldn't break. Not again. After what they'd done to me, I was determined not to repeat the experience. That experience had taken away my fear and left an implacable thing without any definition. Oddly, the workouts became my anchor. Early mornings spent with the trainer, wrapping my knuckles and putting on worn leather gloves, became sacred rituals, the only time that was truly mine. Each punch, every effortful exhalation, was primal and violent, pulsing deep inside. But the anger had changed. The anger had transformed, no longer wild or savage, but now tempered, edgy, ice-cold, and prepared. Mick seemed to sense this shift. He made the jobs miniature; they looked like banal duties at first but contained the baggage of unvoiced wisdom.

Watching over shipments, shadowing men who collected payments, and guarding deliveries were not just tasks. They were drills and exercises for patience and restraint. Mick was instilling in me the notion that strength was not solely about power, but also about control.

"Anger without control is nothing," Mick would declare, his voice unyielding like cold granite, centuries of experience embodied in every word. Those very adjectives infiltrated and embedded themselves in me, like sediment, over time until they became me. The rage within me continued to burn, steady and restrained, awaiting its release. Then came the night when everything changed.

I was alone in the flat; I pushed through the haze of exhaustion after a brutal workout. My muscles ached, my chest heaving as I embraced the silence. Then through the silence came a knock, sharp and deliberate against the door. I opened it to find Paul standing there, his face unreadable, his posture tense. He didn't have to say anything; he never did; instead, he presented me with a folded piece of paper.

"It's from Mick," he whispered, but his voice held something unsaid. His eyes lingered on mine for a beat before he turned and vanished into the darkened hallway. I shut the door, the paper rough against my palms. Mick's rough handwriting sprawled across it in blunt simplicity:

"Are you ready to begin?"

The words fell upon me in the form of a shroud and dense, inescapable weight on my shoulders. This was the culmination of all those hours — all the blood and sweat. Mick had been forging me, shaping me into something relentless. Now he was ready to set me loose. There would be no going back. Paul returned two nights after I received the note. His face was unreadable; unknowing what lay ahead, I jumped into the front seat of his car. The space between us was heavy with silence and understanding, but unarticulated.

This wasn't like the other nights. There was a change in the air, a darker entity below and hidden. We travelled along the street's roads, bathed in the muddy yellow hue cast by the streetlights. Buildings all around us groaned, their facades crumbling and tired. At last, Paul came to a dilapidated building, the windows black, the walls tarnished with years of neglect. He turned off the engine and stared into the broken windscreen for a while before turning to me.

"Mick says this one's on you," he said, his voice steady but weighted. He handed me a battered leather case, the kind you wouldn't look at twice. I flipped it open to show a small blade, the edge barely glowing in the dark. Simple. Efficient. Deadly.

"You know who he is," Paul said, his tone flat.

"Take your time. Make it clean." I didn't need him to elaborate. Mick had chosen Callum Dunne, 'Cal,' from the group of them.

I remembered him clearly. He wasn't the loudest in their group, but he was the cruellest. The viciousness lurking beneath his wiry frame was evident. Cal wasn't as hard as the others, but he took aim and delivered blows that were surgically accurate, choosing his targets with forethought and intent to inflict pain. His face, though boyish, was disfigured by a slight crook in his nose, most likely from a fight long forgotten, and a network of faint scars across his knuckles, souvenirs from the pain he'd inflicted on others. I found him in the back of a grimy pub, his laugh too loud, his presence too big for the narrow booth he occupied.

He had a way of commanding attention. The laughter of his cronies rolled around him like a shield, but I stayed in the shadows, watching, waiting. When he finally stumbled out alone, the dim light revealed the cocky swagger in his step. He walked down a narrow lane, the noise from the pub eventually disappearing in the night. It was muggy, and the sickly-sweet smell of stale beer hung from the walls. My footsteps were careful and unobtrusive as I walked behind him, concealing the blade in my grasp. Cal sensed me too late. He contorted, his pupils shrinking as he searched for the outline of my face in the darkness. Recognition dawned in his eyes just as I stepped into the light.

"You!" he breathed, his voice thick with disbelief.

Startled, Cal's expression instantly deteriorated into something far uglier, instinctive; a defensive smirk wiped across his face. His spindly build straightened as if to dictate power, but his gaze betrayed him. No matter how strong he believed he was, fear lingered within him, a flame that he believed would never fade.

"I don't know what you think you're doing, but you have the wrong guy," he began, his voice wavering slightly. His hand twitched at his side, torn between the instincts of fighting and running.

"Just turn around, mate, and walk away. This doesn't have to get messy." The corner of my mouth twitched, not a smirk anymore, but something close.

"Messy?" I echoed, my voice low and cold.

"This is nothing compared to how you left me that night." Recognition flared again, clearer now. His face paled, the cracks in his bravado widening.

"See," he added, tilting back his hands a bit as if in supplication.

"Whatever happened, I don't even remember. We were just drunk — just messing around, yeah? Boys being boys."

I gripped the blade tightly, the hilt holding me firmly in place as anger and temper threatened to surface. His words were a fucking pathetic attempt at brushing off his involvement, as though a shrug and a grin could undo my shattered jaw, the months of humiliation, and the years of rage.

"Boys being boys?" In some way, my voice exuded a calmness that foreshadows a storm.

"That's what you call it?" The streetlamp overhead projected clean, broken shadows on his own face while he shifted awkwardly.

"I didn't mean..." I cut him off from finishing his sentence. The anger now rising, I threw my fist at him, landing squarely on his jaw. The sound of bone meeting flesh was sharp and satisfying. He fell backward; a curse rolled off his tongue as he spat blood onto the pavement.

"You think I forgot?" I stepped forward, each word measured, deliberate.

"Think I'd let it slide? You broke me that night, Cal. But I'm not the one bleeding now." He lashed out, his movements wild and desperate. His swing was intended to frighten, yet he made no genuine attempt to make contact. I quickly ducked, taking a sidestep, and exacted a swinging blow with my fist clean into the back of his ribcage. The air left his chest in a hissing wheeze as he lunged into the side of the alleyway, fighting to catch his breath. Cal was trying to stabilise himself with one hand.

"You don't have to do this," he wheezed, clutching his side. But his voice lacked conviction. I tilted my head, letting the words sink in, not one ounce of pity. Something smaller and weaker had replaced the predator. He was scrambling now, his footing uneven. For a fleeting instant, I let him swing in a suspended state of panic, enjoying the shift of power.

Then I closed the distance. He struck back desperately, in a sweeping arc, making him extremely vulnerable. I caught his wrist, twisting his arm up his back until he yelped, the blade slipping easily from my free hand into his exposed side. The gasp that followed was wet and ragged. He fell to his knees, and with a flurry of his hands to the site of the wound, blood poured through his fingers.

"You don't get to beg," I said quietly, crouching to meet his gaze. His eyes darted aimlessly between my own, his mouth moving soundlessly, but he was struggling to find the words.

"Remember?" I urged, my voice barely a murmur echoing in the emptiness. He made a weak curtsey, tears spilling down his grimy visage. The contentment that bubbled up inside me was a dark, icy, and complete satisfaction. I wanted to bask in his terror and pain, but instead I leaned in closer.

"This is for me," I said, my tone devoid of emotion, sharp as the edge in my hand.

The blade slid in cleanly, a whisper against flesh. He gave a start once, his pupils going glassy and his limbs held stiff, before falling forward. I held him captive for a second, the pressure of him against me, then released his lifeless form to the floor. The alley was silent save for the soft drip of blood pooling beneath him. The night seemed to hold its breath; the distant hum of the town reduced to a faint echo. I stood over him, staring at the stillness, feeling nothing but the cold clarity of a purpose fulfilled. There was no room for regret, no space for reconsidered action. This was justice brutal, intimate, and final.

The blade remained firmly in my grasp as I wiped it off on his jacket and reinserted it into its original case. The air was cool and damp, but my thinking was clean. I turned around and walked away, leaving him to lie in the darkness.

Every stride was meticulous and deliberate, akin to someone who had crossed the limit. There was no turning back now. One down. There are still four of them left. Had I finished the job? The blade had pierced with a bite, the crimson forming a slow ooze beneath him, while the lightest flicker in his fingers — a faint rasp — breathed against his lips, behind them resonating in a wavering key. Was it the final reflex of a dimming life, or was there something still binding him to the physical world? I didn't check. I couldn't. Either way, it wouldn't matter. For the time being, I reminded myself that Cal might be gone.

Shadows in Alexandria

The wind screeched in the narrow alleys, its shrill, high-pitched scream tearing through the blackness. It carried the fresh scent of the loch from miles away, an unwelcome whisper of cold, unrelenting water. Gusts rattled the fragile glass of the buildings leaning on the street's architecture. Their once — bright façades now dulled and seemed to shiver against the chill, as though even the buildings were fighting to hold on to a version of themselves long since lost.

Alexandria, the place I once called home, seemed off tonight. It was familiar, yes, but in a way that tugged at something deep inside me, a tautness in my chest that quickened my breath. The shadows concealed secrets I hadn't yet discovered and memories I wasn't prepared to confront. Every dark alley and creaking corner felt like a trap, beckoning me back to my former self. I walked purposefully in the freezing wind, my collar turned up against the chill. I buried my hands deep in my hoodie pockets, pressing my fingertips against the hidden knife's edge.

It wasn't comfort I looked for, but clarity. I needed its weight to firm me up against the memories trying to rise from the depths of my gaze. Months had passed since my last walk along these streets, and the boy haunting me remained unchanged. I could feel his shadow flickering at the edges of my vision, fragile, weak, and broken, a ghost of the life I'd left behind. But I wasn't him anymore. They had silenced, beaten, and crushed that boy's spirit, leaving him powerless with a jaw wired shut and wounds too deep to mend.

What haunted these streets now was not a ghost of the past but something harder and more unforgiving. I was here for unfinished business. This was not a nostalgic journey or a pathetic quest for resolution. Tonight, I hunted. This was my second hunt. Ryan 'Rydo' Gibb. His face remained in mind, though time had washed down the borders. He was lanky, was quick on the uptake, and the sudden tips of his tongue, quick and alert, never stopped managing to emit that seeable smear of a sound that sent shivers down your spine. One of the provocateurs, Rydo enjoyed the pain, so his insults did more damage than a beating.

It was his voice I still remember, intense, sarcastic, malice oozing from it. He laughed the loudest that night, his words fuelling the others as they took turns beating me.

Rydo had believed he was untouchable, too clever, and too quick to ever face the consequences of his actions. But tonight, I would prove him wrong. I spotted him in front of one of the oldest pubs in the town, its walls blistered with the age and smoke of the years and stained by the passage of time.

Stale beer and the smell of cigarette butts pressing into the pavement filled the air. The venue was a sanctuary for inhabitants who took refuge in its obscure nooks and crannies like barnacles, drinking their beers as if they held life's secrets behind the windowless building. Rydo leaned against the wall near the alley that led up to the flats, his cigarette dangling loosely from his lips. He exhaled a lazy plume of smoke into the night air, the flickering streetlamp casting a jaundiced light over him. His features were more defined than I can recall, his cheekbones sunken and his skin papery. His face bore the marks of time, and his shoulders exhibited a hint of fatigue.

However, the flicker of what he was still remained, a restless scintillation in the way his eyes darted about at random, searching the darkness as if expecting trouble, yet too proud and arrogant to believe it would ever come to get him. It wasn't trouble he needed to fear; it was me.

I walked towards him in the same style of a ghost, each movement steady and silent. My breath hung before dissolving into the freezing air, my heartbeat steady, my grip firm around the knife in my pocket. He didn't notice me at first, too preoccupied with the glow of his cigarette and the hazy thoughts swirling in his head. It wasn't until I was just a few feet away that he finally looked up, his movements slow and reluctant, as though he sensed the shift in the air but couldn't place its source. Recognition flashed in his face, a split second between the wonder of recollection and the jarring of uncertainty, to anxiety, to the horror of fear. He tried to cover it up with a smile, that the same smug smile that he wore the previous night, laughing at me. His voice trailed in, thick with drink, loud and booming behind the meekest surface of trembling.

"Well, well," he drawled, leaning casually against the wall,

"Look who crawled back from the dead." I didn't answer. Words were useless. They wouldn't change the inevitable. The silence between us stretched, heavy and unyielding. His grin began to falter, replaced by something more uncertain. His gaze darted to the side, searching for an escape, but the alley offered none.

"Jamie, mate," he started, his voice faltering as panic crept into his tone.

"No hard feelings, yeah? I didn't want it to go so far. I didn't think you'd take it so personally." The words struck me sharply, each syllable a reminder of the laughter that had echoed in my ears as it broke me. Rydo had laughed the most, his laughter ringing through the pain haze like a razor. And now he seemed to believe he could write it off, pretend it never did, that I was still the same boy he had left broken on the floor.

The fucking audacity of it made my blood boil. I stepped closer, bridging the gap between us in a single stride. Rydo flinched as I closed the distance. The movement was slight, almost imperceptible. I released the grip on the blade handle and removed my hands from my hoodie. Taking a swing at his smug face, I caught it the first crack in his façade. His muscles contracted, so did a cigarette roll slightly between his thumbs. He tried to cling onto the wall, but I got to him before he could react. I grabbed the scruff of his jacket and slammed him back against the cold brick. The cigarette dropped from his hand and, with a small hissing mechanical sound, landed on the wet ground. His head crashing into the wall, he moaned, his hands scrabbling up into mine, desperate to be free of my hold. But I didn't let go. I moved closer; the breath of my mouth blew in to warm the cold night.

"Is this a joke now?" I snarled, my voice sharp-edged and lethal. He squirmed, his eyes wide with a mixture of fear and defiance.

"C'mon, Mate," he rasped, his tone apprehensive yet channelled through the same brash arrogance.

"It was nothing. Just a laugh. You're taking this way too seriously." The phrase hit a nerve, causing a sharp rush of white-hot rage to course through me. Before I even realised it, my fist connected with his face; the impact was reverberating up my arm. His head shot backwards, and a gush of blood oozed from his nose, staining against the bricks.

"Just a laugh?" I growled, my voice trembling with controlled fury.

"You laughed while you broke me. While you encouraged others to shove that pole into my mouth."

"You and the others made sure I couldn't speak for weeks," I continued. Rydo made a choking sound, his legs flailing in an attempt to get me off him, but Rydo was no match for me.

I slammed him against the wall again, my grip tightening. His gaze fluttered wildly, as fear had all but destroyed the courage he'd tried so hard to be ready with.

"Please," he blurted, pathetic, blood seeping out of the corner of his mouth.

"I... I didn't," Rydo stuttered, but before he could say another word, my fist collided with his cheek, forcing him to be silent. His lip opened wide, and the shrill blood married with the acrid, stale smell of the lane.

My knuckles screamed in protest, the skin raw and stinging, but I didn't care. The pain only fuelled me by sharpening my focus. He wasn't laughing now. I released him, letting his body crumple to the ground.

He collapsed in a heap, his breathing coming in desperate, shallow gulps. His hands shook as he tried to push himself up, but his arms buckled, and he collapsed again, coughing and sputtering. Seeing him defeated, mangled, and helpless in the battle should have resulted in my triumph. Rather, it did not just enlarge the abyss of darkness within me.

I crouched and grabbed a fistful of his jacket and pulled him up so that our faces were inches apart. His bloodshot eyes locked with mine, and within them, I witnessed the full impact of his terror.

"You'll live, for now," I whispered, my voice steady and cold.

"And you'll never forget this. Every time you breathe, every time you look in the mirror, you'll think of me. You'll know this isn't over." His mouth moved soundlessly, a broken attempt at words, but nothing came out. I pushed him away; his head bounced a little on the concrete. He didn't try to get up this time. The fight had vanished. I stood over him, my fists throbbing, my breath heavy. Air around us was still, the distant roar of the town almost inaudible over the crinkling of his breath. He sighed quietly, hunkering into himself as blood settled around his body.

I turned and walked away, my steps deliberate, each one carrying me further from the wreckage I'd left behind. The cold wind howled down the alleyway between the shops, scraping against exposed flesh on my face, but I felt nothing at all. The Main Street stretched out before me, silent and empty. The adrenaline that had powered me started to subside, replaced by an uncanny, still sense of clarity. The fury was past, but there remained a blistery, cold, implacable will.

This was just the beginning. The other three would feel it too. Their faces loomed in my mind: Lee, Ross, Scars. They had joked with Rydo and Cal, mocking me as they had taken turns beating me. They had the idea that they could leave it behind and forget it all.

But I wouldn't let them. One by one, they would learn. There was no escape, no corner of Alexandria or beyond that would keep them safe. I would find them all. I would have them feel the effects of their choices. The wind screamed at my back, and a few soft drops of blood fell off my knuckles. The town centre streets of Alexandria would never be the same for me, and for them too.

The Next Move

Dense fog overtook the streets of Alexandria that night and engulfed the town in an opaque grey smoke. It coated walls and lamp posts, covering the entire town in one of those heavy hazy mists, smearing the lines of the streets as well, warping reality. Behind the smoke, the pallid halo of streetlights struggled to pierce through, their soft, outsized circle creating uncanny, limber shadows that lengthened and contorted as if the fog were alive and voracious, swallowing the town one street corner at a time.

It was a night of shadows, secrets festering, and the air heavy with the expectations of years of shadowed and unconfessed wrongs to be made right. I stood on the curb, my collar turned up to shield against the biting chill that seeped into my bones. Each breath brought with it the appearance and disappearance of a pale cloud of mist. Excitation within me was similar to a spring that was wound up, muscles tensed, nerves humming with purpose. This wasn't just another night. It was now one step closer to encircling the necks of those who thought they had escaped my punishment.

Upfront, a soft buzz of a motor was approaching from a distance, accompanied by a clear tone and a sonorous crescendo that slowly throbbed the boundaries of where I stood. Just a second later, twin headlights appeared, bringing fabulous shafts of light into the gloom. I blinked away from the glare as a black van rolled up next to me, its engine stopping with a muffled roar. The driver's side window retracted with a low whirring, smooth mechanical sound, and in the gloom, Paul presented as a vague shape of tension and anxiety. He just made one brief nod to me, and his face remained, of course, completely unreadable.

We didn't exchange any words; they weren't necessary. We understood why I was present and understood too that

I was prepared. I pushed the door open and dove into the driver's seat, where the cold veil of mist crept over me and enveloped the van following me like an unwanted visitor. The air was filled with unhappiness, as acrid cigarette smoke lingered in the van, accompanied by a distinct smell of gasoline, both wet and damp. It was not a strange smell; it was an occupational reminder of my journey, my decisions, and things I couldn't undo. Paul leaned forward, his movements efficient and unhurried as he shifted the van into gear. Tires whispered over the slick street surface as we rolled off the curb, dissolving into the swirling fog. His gaze remained fixed on the road ahead, his shoulders gripped by the weight of the responsibilities that lay ahead.

We didn't speak. The silence was not disagreeable; it was dense, thick with a silent understanding. Paul had been here before, driving me away after my first target, his expression a hard mask that betrayed nothing. But tonight felt different. Tonight, something in me had shifted. That anger, which had once driven me, now bubbled just beneath the surface, contained and honed into an icy, pinpoint instrument. This wasn't just about revenge anymore. It was a journey of regaining control, proving to them and to myself that I was no longer their powerless victim.

For what felt like hours, we drove through the fog — shrouded streets of Alexandria. The area unfolded around us like a crumbling mausoleum, its narrow roads lined with darkened flats that sagged under the weight of neglect. The fog blurred their sharp angles, and the buildings became dark monoliths silhouetted against the empty streets below. That we would be transported between what is and what is not, real and unreal, was the feeling. Anything outside the van's windows became a mixture of blurry images, with shapes blending together as the darkening sky became thicker and thicker.

At last Paul spoke in a quiet, steady voice, without disturbing the quietness.

"Mick has the lead," he spoke in a steady voice, looking straight ahead.

"Your man's been spotted down by Sweeney's. He's laying low, but he can't hide forever." My heart pounded faster, a dull stroke reverberating through my chest. I knew exactly who Paul meant. Liam 'Lee' Sutherland. The memory of him was imprinted in my brain, as sharp as the jagged black tattoo that spiralled up around his neck like a vicious vine. He was the most savage of them — his savagery was not veiled but paraded around as a mark of prestige.

I could still hear the sound of his laughter, mean and instinctual, as he tossed me onto the ground that night, his tattooed wrists pinning me brutally to the ground while he teased me for my inadequacy. Lee had relished it, the power he held, the way I couldn't fight back. He had savoured each and every moment, each and every hit, each and every insult. He headed it, his voice dominating while he sneered at me. The picture of his face came into my head, warped by evil, the line of his smirk clouded by the dusk of memory. However, the roles would reverse tonight. Tonight, it was his turn to be powerless.

"When?" I rasped; the words caught in my molars. Paul glanced at me; his expression unreadable.

"Soon," he replied.

"He's there most nights. We'll drive by and make sure he's alone. Once we stop... there's no going back." I nodded, gripping the edge of the seat rest with my fingertips. Anger ran rampant in my body; it was hot and bitter but also something cold and clearly defined. I was ready. The days and weeks since my last encounter had felt like a countdown, each moment leading me closer to this. Its journey through the gear smithing of Mick, the command, the sanguine, and the ocular tissues, through the marrow, the lessons, and the blood and tears has been leading to tonight.

Now, the culmination of everything was in sight. The van abruptly stopped, and both Paul and I immediately began searching for him. As the van approached the jetty, the engine provided a soft hum. The fog here was thickest; it swirled along the riverbank at all angles, smothering the neglected shoreline and derelict boats on the waterfront like a living grave. The air was crisper, more stinging; Paul gently slowed the van to a stop a few meters from the carpark exit, keeping all of us in the dark. He slunk forward, and his piercing eyes pierced the mist. Over there, he muttered, nodding towards a weak light at the far end of the bridge. I followed his gaze, my eyes narrowing against the gloom. At first, the light was all I could see, a dim, irregular glow that barely pierced the shadows.

But then, as the fog shifted, I saw him. Liam 'Lee' Sutherland. He slouched over, contorted on his back on the floor against a crate with a very faint, light orange filtered from the streetlights above. He carried himself in an easy, almost slack manner, as if he had no worries at all. But already, in the simple scintillation of light, I saw the burden on his shoulders; he was still barely moving. He appeared to be attempting to blend into the shadows and become invisible, but the tattoo on his neck betrayed him. Its black, twisted lines unfurled across his body, bold against the white demarcation of the neck. For him, it served as a symbol, akin to a milestone, a tribute to the sorrow he had caused. The sight of him sent a jolt through me, part anger, part something colder and darker.

He didn't know I was here. He did not know that the boy he left, bruised and bleeding, was in fact just a few meters away. Paul's voice broke the silence, low and steady.

"He's been staying down here somewhere close by, hiding out. But tonight..." He left the words unfinished, a barely perceptible smirk playing at the corner of his lips. Nodding, I felt the full weight of it all. This was different from the others. The first two hadn't known I was coming. I ambushed them, leaving them stumbling hard and bloodied in the dark.

But Lee... he knew someone was coming for him; at least, he felt as if somebody was hunting him. He knew his time was running out. The tension in his posture, the way he melted into the fog like prey trying to evade a predator — it was all there, written in his every move.

Paul turned to me, his eyes sharp, assessing.

"You go in alone," he said, his voice flat but heavy with meaning.

"Mick needs to know if you're ready to finish this on your own." I met his gaze and nodded. This wasn't about the job; it was a test, a trial. Mick asked whether I would be able to take it all the way without hesitating, unbroken, and be there at the end without being held by someone else. I reached for the glove compartment and got a pair of black gloves. The leather felt old and rough against my skin, and the act of putting them on grounded me. Without another word, I pushed the van door open. The cold air touched my face, but I welcomed it.

The haze surrounded me as I came in amongst the darkness that shrouded everything and brought it to the status of black and silence. I followed Lee into the underpass, mannered for all the intents and purposes, tunnel like, very dark, and very narrow. The dim light at the end became brighter with every stride I made, leading me on. My boots produced soundlessly the measured passage on the wet pavement, each one deliberate, intended. I turned once to glance back at the van. Through the windscreen, Paul's face was barely visible, his eyes never leaving me.

He made a tiny nod but then focused on the fog again. I turned to face forward, my heart going steady in my chest. Every step I took brought me closer to him. I was getting closer to Lee, the one who had held me down, laughed, sneered at my pain, and left me to die. Lee was lost in his own thinking, a cigarette now in his hand casting a pale, thin beam of light upwards, which then dispersed a ghostly plume of smoke into the starless night sky. Lee, with his head bowed and shoulders hunched, exuded a sense of security. He wasn't safe. I ducked into the shadows, my form disappearing into the black world as I narrowed the gap between us. Anger inside me was built into a tool, and under restraint, it sharpened. I didn't rush. I wanted to produce that sensation at the very moment of recognition, when he realised what was about to pass.

Lee, suddenly startled by my presence, looked up at last. His eyes widened as they met mine, confusion flickering across his face before giving way to recognition.

"Jamie," his voice stunned and hushed, barely audible over the steady lap of water against Balloch Bridge.

I didn't give him time to say anything else. In one fluid movement, I bridged the distance between us. My hand shot out in a grab for him from the front of his body and pulled him to the ground; then his back hit a low wall, a boulder, or a large rock. He fought, his hands raking the air against me, but I was now stronger. His wide view locked onto mine, and there it was: the fear, the huddling, the snap of recognition. He wouldn't shy away from it.

"Thought you could hide from me?" I hissed, my voice low and venomous.

"Thought you could run from what you did?" He coughed out a word and a half; I made him stop sputtering. My grip tightened around his throat, silencing him, the anger inside me boiling over into something raw and unstoppable. This wasn't just revenge. This was justice. And tonight, Lee would pay.

No Escape

Flinging my arm back, I drove my fist forward, connecting hard with his face. The force sent him tumbling backward, his head cracking against the ground with a hollow, brutal thud that echoed through the narrow underpass. The sound reverberated in the moist air, a ghostly echo that slowly disappeared below creeping fog. The sound was subtle, causing you to squirm beneath your skin, yet it was particularly satisfying tonight.

His pupils dilated suddenly in shock and fear, and the dreadful insight struck him like a blow to the abdomen. I could see blood and sweat on his forehead, glistening under the dim, flickering streetlamp that cast murky light over the underpass. His eyes scanned wildly back and forth in a desperate attempt to find an escape — something or anything that could save him. But we both knew the truth. There was no escape. His breath came in sharp, shallow gasps, each more desperate than the last. His expression was that of a cornered animal, wild and frantic, slowly realising that his options had been exhausted. I stood over him, watching in silence as the fear sank in, postponing its inevitability.

"Please," he stammered, almost inaudible as nervousness shook his voice, trying to be heard above the choking silence.

"It — it wasn't meant for you." The final word pressed out of his mouth, choked with despair. A sound of dry, unfeeling mirth left me, a shard of metal cutting through the mist. What the fuck does he mean? It wasn't meant for me, and it was in the same pitiful tone as the others trying to absolve themselves, as if words alone could erase the scars they'd carved into me.

He wasn't sorry. None of them had been fucking sorry when they held me down, smashing my jaw, leaving me broken and bleeding like I was nothing more than trash.

"Wasn't intended for me," I growled through gritted teeth, soft but edged like a blade.

"What the fuck do you mean, you left me to die?" I walked toward him, seizing hold of his collar and pulling him forward until his face was right in my space. I wanted him to perceive the fire in my gaze; he wanted to sense the extent of the fury that it had caused. His pale, sweat — slicked face twisted in terror, a thin smear of blood streaking down his temple. His whole body shook with desperation, radiating from it like a beacon in the dark.

"You think it wasn't meant for now?" I whispered, my tone laced with malice. He shook his head rapidly and joltingly, convulsing, his lips quivering as he struggled to say anything. No words came out. His terror was tangible, a thing around us in the thick, stuffy air of the river.

One of his hands twitched weakly, as though he might raise it to defend himself or plead for mercy. I didn't give him the chance. With a flash, I threw him against a pallet behind him. The effect was strong, resonating through the wooden slats and echoing a choked sound out of his mouth. His head snapped back, his body sagging slightly, dazed. He was starting to crumble. I pulled him forward again, dragging him deeper into the underpass, out of the reach of the faint light streaming through the opening.

His legs barely held him, stumbling with each forced step. His breathing came in short, shallow bursts, and I could feel the panic radiating off him, a suffocating stench of fear that mingled with the damp, sour air. He spoke in a rambling, nonsensical way — a chain of partially formed words and apologies falling from his mouth in a jumbled flow of words. Each word was a weak, futile attempt to pacify me, to stop what was coming. I pushed him to the wall with a clatter, the impact creating a sharp crack like noise. He winced, his face grimacing in pain while he struggled for air, his chest rapidly rising and falling unevenly.

I snarled, my voice piercing through his mumbling like a knife. He went rigid, his dilated, wide, frightened eyes fixing on the irises of the other. His face was a disaster, blood running from his nose, his lip split, and bruising already starting to form across his fair skin. His entire body trembled, every shallow breath a struggle.

"You think I'm here to talk?" I asked, each word deliberate, heavy with menace.

"You think I'm here to forgive?" He reached for his mouth, a hesitant utterance escaping from the back of his throat, but I prevented him from finishing.

My clenched fist shot forward, slamming into his stomach with a force that jolted through my arm. He doubled over, with a choked gasp erupting from him while air cascaded out of his lungs. His knees bent, but I pulled him straight back up at the last minute, delivering another spurt of force to his side. This time, I felt something give a faint crack beneath my knuckles. He emitted a piteous cry, gripping at his side as his body crumpled inward. However, my work was far from over. I seized him by the neck and pulled him to a sitting position upright. His limbs almost failed him, his whole form rippling against the wall like a rag doll caught in a gale. Blood ran from the tip of his nose and left cheek, accumulating at the chin, and then ran down onto his ripped shirt.

His glazed eyes darted around wildly, clouded with terror, his mouth working soundlessly as though trying to summon words that refused to come. I leaned in, my voice a low, steely note that pierced through his fog of dread.

"You're going to feel everything I felt that night," I said, each word slow, deliberate, and cutting.

"Every fucking second of it." He whimpered, a pitiful, broken sound that only fuelled the cold resolve surging through me. His trembling hands spasmed weakly on either side of him, a pathetic attempt to scare me that now held no significance.

He was disintegrating, hopeless to bear the weight of the terror that hung between us, crushing him with the knowledge of what was ahead. I simply released him, observing as his body collapsed onto the damp and unclean path. He hunched in on himself, clutching his battered ribs, his gasps for air coming in short, choppy pants that sounded less like breathing and more like cries.

"Please... I didn't..." he croaked, his voice raw and fractured.

"It wasn't..." The words faded into a deep, guttural moan as he gripped to his side, and the pain engulfed him. I kneeled with my eye on him as his wandering eyes miraculously focused on me. There was no rage in me now, no need to shout or scream. The anger had turned to ashes, only leaving something colder, more rational behind.

"Do you think begging is going to save you?" I asked, my voice soft, almost mocking.

"Do you think I didn't beg that night? Do you think I didn't plead for you all to stop?" His head shook weakly, his lips parting as if to answer, but no sound came. His wide, tear-filled eyes met mine, and I saw it — the moment of realisation, as it finally dawned on him. He understood now. This wasn't a fight. This was an execution, a judgement for what he had caused. I straightened, watching as he made a feeble attempt to crawl away.

His broken body dragged across the ground, each movement a struggle. He managed to pull himself a few feet before collapsing onto his side, his chest heaving, his face twisted in agony. I took a step forward, narrowing the distance between us, while he leapt back at my silhouette. A pitiful sound escaped his lips, his eyes darting around in a desperate, futile search for escape. But there was none. He was alone, just as I had been. I got down again, crouching further and drawing closer to whisper in his direction.

"You'll remember this night," I murmured, my tone steady and venomous.

"You'll remember what it feels like to be powerless." He shook, his body quivering as I stomped on his side, the full weight of my body connecting with his as a hollow, cracked sound came out of him. His hands clutched at his ribs, his shoulders shaking as the weight of his fear consumed him. His wide, panicked eyes stared into the void, searching for salvation that would never come. I straightened again, fixing my eye on him as he lay sprawled on the hard, damp ground.

For a short time, I thought about completing it, crushing his pain in the final shot. But that would have been too easy. Too merciful. No, I wanted him to live with this. He should bear the weight of this night, each moment serving as a constant reminder of his own helplessness. I wanted the memory to haunt him, to claw at him every time he closed his eyes.

Without a word, I kicked my boot into the back of his head. His skull tilted to the side with impact — a bang, a sickening crunch echoing in the arches of the bridge. He sighed a gurgle, his body convulsing once and then folding into the sidewalk with a thud.

The fog pressed in upon us, drowning out the empty moan that left his mouth as he sank deeper into the earth. I stared at him for a second, my chest rising and falling normally, my breathing noticeable in the fresh air. He did not move; only the slightest movement from his fingers was the only indication that Lee was alive.

I knew he was finished; I turned and walked away, the sound of his broken sobs fading into the thick fog that swallowed the night. The cold, dense air pressed against me, but I kept going. Each step I took felt lighter, freer, as though the chains that had bound me for so long were finally starting to loosen. The small village of Balloch loomed around me, its darkened streets stretching out in endless, empty silence. The fog engulfed me as a living being; it hushed the entire world, and only the quiet thud of my footsteps filled the air.

This wasn't over. Not by a long shot. I still had two to face. The others wouldn't escape their reckoning. They would feel it too. Individually, they would experience what it felt like to look directly into the abyss of their creation. They would have the crushing weight of their actions on their shoulders, squeezing them, crushing them, just like I had. As I disappeared into the shadows, the sound of his suffering faded behind me, swallowed by the night. Never again would it be the same for him, and never again for me.

Quiet Between
Storms

Dawn crept upon Alexandria like a reluctant promise, dull and grey, casting weak light that stretched long shadows over the stone buildings as the fog slowly began to lift. The air that morning was cold, heavy, and dense, saturated with mist clinging to the corners of the streets and the cocked eaves of the buildings, unwilling to disperse. I waited by the window, and my breath fogged the pane in random areas. Outside the window, the town flowed in low, grey tones, its edges blurred by the smog. The daylight was weak and fuzzy, forming reluctant puddles that vanished as soon as they appeared.

Sleep hadn't come that night, not that I'd expected it to. My knuckles throbbed, raw and swollen, each pulse a reminder of what I'd done. The throbbing pain in my hands was an unwelcome visitor, locked into itself, so I would never forget the brutality I inflicted. I could still hear the sickening crunch from his skull, the sharp noise that pierced through the deadly silence of one unforgiven kick. The memory is on repeat in my head, his great, frightened eyes burning through every pulse of my own. His confidence had completely evaporated, leaving him reduced to a pitiful whimper.

I had made sure of it. However, the satisfaction and sense of vindication I had been seeking were absent. However, the barren, empty space where I imagined revenge would take root had, instead, become filled with an icy, empty ache in the pit buried deep within. I flexed my fingers, flinching as the motion strained against the bruised and swollen surface. It was a prickly sensation, like a tactile tether to my realisation of choice. It had been necessary; I told myself again. Yes, it had been brutal, but it was necessary. Those words had become my refrain, my flimsy weapon to deflect the pain of what I had become.

They had abandoned me to die, laughing as they crushed my jaw, as they drove that cold metallic tube between my lips. They had disgraced me, destroyed me, and instilled in me the feeling of nothingness. Last night, I had returned the favour. I have shown to him at least that same hopelessness, that same soul-destroying terror.

But here in the grey morning light, the triumph I had imagined felt more like ash in my mouth. I stepped back from the window, letting the curtain fall back over me. The flat felt smaller somehow, the walls pressing inward as though the weight of my choices had a physical presence, a mass that filled the empty spaces. Every room I walk through is heavier, and the quiet is almost unbearable. The street was empty, roads were silent, and the air felt like a wispy veil rising from ground level.

Faint echoes of the town sprang to life, accompanied by the metallic clang of a gate and the distant hum of an engine, yet it all seemed distant, like a world I no longer belonged to. Alexandria had been a location where I felt rooted — a location where I could walk its squares without a second thought, confident I belonged. But that was a long time ago. Now it felt foreign, hostile, as though the town itself had turned its back on me.

For a fleeting moment, I wondered if there was still a way out. I longed to escape this path before it engulfed me. However, the idea vanished swiftly, overwhelmed by the weight of everything I'd accomplished. There was no going back. My fate was sealed the moment I threw that first punch. Revenge had become my tether, the only thing that propelled me on. It served as my sole objective and the driving force behind my actions.

Even as I gripped tightly, I sensed its pull, pulling me deeper into the abyss and away from my true self. Every act of violence, every fracture inflicted, was eroding the edges of who I was, until all that was left was this numb, empty, unrecognisable me.

The day lay out in front of me, formlessly and endlessly, each hour slipping into the next in a tedious progression toward an unidentifiable goal. I wandered aimlessly from room to room, with a certain heartbeat like a flat, repetitive, cosmic thread, searching for an object that long ago vanished. Finally, I couldn't stand the stillness any longer. Taking my jacket, I threw it on and went out into the crisp air of a cold morning.

The fog muffled the streets, damp and smothering, encasing the toen in an uncoloured shroud. I walked through known streets, each step reverberating off the slick road surface; each direction was a varied and unpredictable path; each stride was monotonous yet reliable.

Ghosts of memory lurked everywhere I looked, as if they were phantoms. There was the old pub we would go to drink, the shop we would go to on a nice day, and the park where we would spend hours toasting each other's beans. They felt like relics from another life, fragments of a story that no longer belonged to me. I walked for what felt like hours, and the town grew up all around me in a haze of half remembered futures and present-day silhouettes. It wasn't long before I was standing over Loch Lomond, all its beauty stretched out before me when I finally stopped, its surface smooth and unbroken, reflecting the grey sky like a tarnished mirror. The silence was absolute — the sort that sat on your skin.

I stood at the water's edge, staring at the endless expanse of grey, my thoughts scattered and heavy. Revenge had seemed so clear and righteous. They'd hurt me, humiliated me, and broken me. I used to say to myself, in order to have a full life, I have to do it this way, and the pain is the only way I will be rewarded with completion. But it wasn't. Their pain did not obliterate the hollowness in my bones, body, and mind. It hadn't erased the helplessness I'd felt that night; it had given me back the pieces of myself they had taken.

In fact, it only had widened the chasm, hewing it out still until there was nothing but white space. A breeze ran across the loch, causing soft waves across the placid surface and calming the water. I tightly closed my eyes and inhaled a sudden wave of unnaturally cold air, accompanied by a wet sensation that enveloped my entire body, causing a nauseating and stinging shift.

For a fleeting second, I let my mind wander, and I imagined the carefree adolescent I used to be — the one who walked these streets light-heartedly and with a completely unbothered demeanour, a malleable boy who literally believed in being one of the greater things in the world, trusting too easily and expecting the best outcome of every situation. That boy felt like a stranger now, a ghost haunting the edges of my memory. He was a stranger who I could barely remember, overshadowed by the being that had become my projection — a being twisted by pain and sharpened by rage.

Hands, raw and bruised, bore the evidence of that change. The jagged scabs and swollen knuckles were symbols of what I'd done and what I could never undo. These were not in the hands of the child anymore — the innocent child. These hands belonged to a criminal, capable of crossing unbreakable boundaries. The idea made my back shudder, but it wasn't remorse. It was acceptance. This was who I was now. The boy I once was has vanished, buried beneath the burden of my experiences. In his place was someone colder, harder, a weapon sharpened by rage and shaped by vengeance.

That emptiness was huge, but it was mine now, like my scars. body. By the time I got back to the flat, the day had faded into twilight. Above, the sky darkened to a sombre grey, the street enveloped in dark as the last of the light left. The stifling silence of the place encased me at each footstep.

The room was dark but that is what I expected when I entered the flat, the routine sound of the latch resonating throughout the quietness of the flat. I cast my jacket off and hung it on the wall by the door, my steps slow and purposeful, burdened by a pressing weight so heavy and pervasive as it settled above me. Moving to the little table next to the window, I fell into the worn chair heavily, allowing its creak to pierce its silence. The lamppost at the corner wobbled weakly, and it cast dim, long, slender shadows that crossed the walls. I sat in the semi darkness, my eyes fixed on the window, though I wasn't really looking at anything.

The glass reflected back my own blurred image, fragmented, and distorted by the faint glow of the outside light. My thoughts turned, unbidden, to the others. Paul. Mick. The head men who took me under their wing, who had led me when I was lost, trained, and guided me, laying out the codes of a world I never knew existed.

They'd tempered me, let me see what it took to make it in a world in which strength and fealty were the only currencies that counted. I had blindly put my trust in them, had let them mold me into the person I was. They had removed my fear and my reluctance and bedrock me into something unbreakable or so I had believed. However, being in the dark now, I had to wonder, to what extent, my own choice had been and how much simply had it been allowed to befall me. Piece by piece, I had already given parts of myself over to another, until all that was left was this person, consumed by the singular drive to revenge. It wasn't just for me anymore. It was for every scar they'd left on my body, every night I'd spent lying awake, haunted by the memory of what they'd done. It was for the boy I used to be, the one they had destroyed. The thought flickered briefly before fading, replaced by the cold certainty that had driven me this far.

There was no use looking back. The route that I was on did not end and I was unable to take a reverse turn. Out there, both of them, they were still living, unchanged, unaffected by their catastrophic choice, unaware that they would be put through the mill. Not for long. I slumped back in my chair, and shut my eyes, allowing the silence to permeate me completely. The emptiness I'd experienced before had been replaced by something sterner, more steadfast. The worries and 'what ifs' all festered, gone and passing way replaced by the grim determination that got me to this point.

My breathing was normal, the pain that now battered my knuckles was a dull, rhythmic beat that corresponded with my heartbeat. Away from my thoughts the environment blurred into a sharp focus, as darkness draped over me like a sheet. This was my life now, a life built on pain and vengeance, where each act of violence brought me closer to the end I looked for. I had made peace with it, accepted it as the price I had to pay. And in that instant, as the dark enmeshed itself completely around me, there came a kind of strange peace. It wasn't, peace as most people would imagine it to be, but it was, sufficient. It was the calm before the hurricane, clear in my mind what needed to be done, there was no stopping, there was no turning back.

A Lesson in Loyalty

The knock came in the middle of the night, sharp and unwelcome, cutting through the silence of the flat like a knife. I had been fast asleep in the armchair by the window, dreaming of peace and in the distant, a muffled roar of the town beyond, while my mind continued to spin with what happened over the last few days. However, that knock sprung me from sleep, my heart beating in my breast as I fixated downward into the blackness. I didn't need to look through the peephole I knew who would be standing there.

I pulled myself from the chair, every step slow and measured, feeling the weight of what lay on the other side of the door. Mick didn't knock without reason; if he was here, there was purpose in it, a message waiting for me that wouldn't come lightly. I swung the door wide open, and he stood there, his large format outlining in the unwelcoming phosphorescence of the hallway, his dark raincoat cinched tight across his frame with the upturned collar against the blackness. His face was half hidden in shadow, but his eyes held a weight I hadn't seen before a heaviness that seemed to add years to him, making him look older, worn. He went -silent, and without a sound, into the siting flat, exam-in-ing the room with his eyes, taking it all in at once, vestibuling each and every one of the details in a curt glance. There wasn't much to see just a worn armchair by the window, a small table cluttered with empty bottles and ashtrays, shadows clinging to every corner. It was a place stripped of warmth, barely more than four walls and a roof. Yet, somehow, Mick looked as though he knew exactly where he was, as though he'd always known where to find me if he needed to.

"Late at night," I muttered, shutting the door behind him, leaning against it as I watched him carefully. I didn't trust him out of my sight for even a second. Mick gave a short nod, moving to the centre of the room, his hands slipping into the pockets of his coat as he continued to survey the place.

"Late nights are a part of this life," he murmured, almost to himself, in a hushed, contemplative tone that announced experience.

"Sleep doesn't come easy when there's blood on your hands." The words hung between us, charged with a weight that was impossible to ignore. I wasn't sure whether he was talking to me or to himself, but I did not interrupt. I let it stay, watching as they flailed in the depths of his mind. His gaze seemed distant at first, lost somewhere I couldn't follow. However, he immediately looked at me, present on every level, his dark eyes steady, unblinking. There was no question of the keenness of his gaze, of that sharpness which slices through any lingering disbeliefs.

"You've done well," he said, his tone steady, deliberate.

"Better than I thought you would."

The words hit me in a way I hadn't anticipated, stirring a strange mix of pride and unease that I couldn't quite sort out. I wasn't doing it for kudos, but it came from Mick, and it carried the weight of those words that I couldn't turn away. This was the fellow who had deconstructed me to my raw essence, stripped away all that was flimsy, and moulded me into steel with a serrated edge.

However, you must know there is one thing you need to understand, he added, voice hardening, the metal under his words unmistakable.

"This path you're walking — it's not just about revenge. It's about loyalty. It's about understanding where you are and who to believe in."

I nodded, feeling the effect of his statement on my spine. Mick's loyalty wasn't something freely given. It had to be earned, and even then, it came with strings attached strings you often didn't notice until you were already too deep to turn back.

He moved closer, his eyes fixed on mine, the force of that gaze too great to refuse to notice. It was not just an image, it was a provocation, arousing me to take the mantle of saying everything that he was conveying.

"I don't take just anyone under my wing," he said, his voice low but firm, every word deliberate.

"And I don't give loyalty for free. You've earned your place here, but it comes with a price. You understand that, don't you?"

The question hung in the mist, public but private in the way of phrases. I locked eyes with him, sensing the weight of his words and the solemn authority that he seemed to wear as a second skin. Mick wasn't just a crime boss; he was a master of control, a man who had built his empire on loyalty and fear, on the unbreakable bonds he forged with those who served him. And now, standing here in the dim, shadowed silence of my flat, I could feel that same bond tightening around me, a leash I hadn't noticed until it was already pulled taut.

"I understand," I said, my voice steady, each word carrying the unspoken vow I'd made the moment I chose this life.

Mick, however, only made a quick nod a picture of approval in his gaze, yet what concealed under it was a deeper feeling. It was a near fatherly sentiment, but in an indirect manner, a mixture of pride and portent as he looked over me.

"Good," he said softly.

"Loyalty isn't just about following orders. It's about becoming more than a tool. It's about figuring out the influence, the world and when to act," He moved away, but always looking at me, the weight of his words grounding me, burying me like some absolute, inescapable truth that I wished it wasn't the case, but that I could neither escape nor run from no matter how much I craved to.

"This world is not for the faint of heart," Mick said, his voice even, but penetrating, a whisper of menace tightened in each utterance.

"You've learned that better than most. However, if you mean to survive — if you mean to be more than just another washed up face in a blur of shattered kids, you have to make something you couldn't forget."

There was something rough in his tone, but not cruel. It had the same weight as a teacher's lessons, sharp and necessary. For a moment, I saw a flicker of something else in his expression an odd warmth, rough around the edges but undeniable. It was a literal shock to watch Mick like this, and the faint echo of something that was close to sympathy. He was, always, a central figure of authority, one who to be obeyed, he demanded, and to convince whom he alone should be listened to. But there was also now in his proclamation the other, the Fatherly sound. A mentor, yes, but also a man who saw himself reflected in me.

"Why me?" I blurted the question out before I could think to stop it, the words uncensored and raw. Mick's gaze didn't waver, but something dark crossed his face, an emotion I couldn't quite read. He momentarily took his eyes off of the person and looked between his monitor and the window, fixated on its width then a fixed piece of the sky beyond, as if in the emptiness he watched even beyond their presence with the world as though he could encounter it in the black somewhere in the depth, unaware that no one else would.

For a moment, he was silent, his hands still buried in his coat pockets, his posture as composed as ever, but there was a heaviness in the air between us.

"Because I perceive something within you," he finally said, voice no longer roaring, but almost caring.

"Something I haven't seen in a long time." Turning back to me he fixed his eyes on me in a steady gaze, unblinking, the intensity of his stare rendering me breathless.

"You've got fire, kid. But you've also got control. That's rare, rarer than you realise. The majority of those who embark on such a course burn themselves to a cinder. They succumb, get lost in the rage, in the catastrophe. But you…" He paused, studying me as if trying to measure the truth of his own words.

"You've learned how to hold the fire without letting it destroy you."

His words landed hard, resonating deep within me. I'd spent so much of my life wrestling with my anger, trying to keep it from swallowing me whole. I had levelled it, sharpened it and made it a weapon I could use for defence rather than have it kill me. And now, hearing Mick say it aloud, it felt like he was putting words to something I had always known but never utterly understood. He had seen it, recognised it, and chosen me because of it.

But there was something else in the way he looked at me, something that sent a chill through my chest. Beneath his words, beneath the recognition and the praise, there was a darker undertone, a glimmer of possession. Mick didn't just see me as a protégé. He saw me as part of himself, an extension of his empire, a reflection of his own strength. It was both unnerving and oddly compelling.

"Well, there's a choice," Mick said, his breath an unheard, steady but constant deep drone every sound of raw musing.

"Run from all this nonsense, just disappear into the BACKGROUND, just one more faceless nobody. Or you can stay and become something more. But if you stay, you follow my rules. My way. You become part of this world, part of my team."

The finality in his words hit like a sharp blow, cold and unyielding. There was no debate, there was no negotiation. Mick wasn't just offering me a path; he was claiming me, binding me to his world, his rules, his power. And part of me, the part that craved strength and control, the part that wanted to rise above the helplessness I'd once known, wanted that more than anything. I wanted to be bigger than myself, to be something stronger, sharper, untouchable. But another part of me felt the weight of it, the chains that came with loyalty to Mick, with stepping fully into his world. Mick stepped back, the sharpness in his eyes softening just slightly, the faintest hint of a smile tugging at the corners of his mouth.

"Just think about it, lad," he remarked, casual now.

"There's no rush. But just know this you're not alone. You've got people who would stand by you, who would fight for you. That's more than most in this world can say."

It, he turned his heel and walked to the door, each step purposeful, the impact of his weight against the warped floorboards tangible. He did not look back and opened the door and went into the poorly lit hallway. The sound of the door being closed behind him, leaving me to stop in my tracks, his statement floating there like mist. I stayed there for a moment, staring at the closed door, the stillness of the flat settling around me like a shroud. Mick's presence was gone, but the weight of his offer remained, heavy and suffocating. I sank back into the chair by the window, my thoughts churning, pulling me in every direction. Mick didn't just give me a way, a mission, but with it came chains

I haven't until this minute perceived. His love, his protection, wasn't free and it bound me to him, his power, his life.

At the same time, while I sat in the dark, it drew me, the dark temptation of power and belonging. For so long, I'd been clawing my way back from the edge, searching for something to hold onto, something to make me feel whole again. And here was Mick, offering me everything I thought I wanted a family, a purpose, a place where I fit. But it wasn't without a price. The night went on, the blackness surrounding me, and I knew, with a dreadful certainty, that the lie settles in my chest. The choice was mine, yes. But in my heart, I already knew which path I would take. There was no turning back now. I was no longer just a boy seeking retribution. I was something else something darker.

And the price, whatever it was, was one I was willing to pay.

Shadows of Home

The light of morning diffused through the frame of the blind's, streaks formed of painted broken shapes, onto the walls of the flat. Shadows lengthened and moved as I bent forward over the top of the chair by the window, elbows griping over the knees tightly. The stillness in the room felt oppressive, each movement stirring the air just enough to remind me of how lifeless everything had become.

The flat was cold, a deep chill that the coarse fabric of my duvet couldn't keep at bay. The pallid light made the room appear washed out, ghostly, as if it had also succumbed to the emptiness pressing in on me. Silence went very heavy and persistent in the air, not simply no sound, but a physical pressure pushing in from all sides. It had been days since Mick's visit.

Weeks had passed since his pronouncements had set about delaminating layers of anger and adrenaline and prompting me to deal with the world of which I had created. Working up a sweat and against the backdrop of grappling and the impact, it was very easy to ignore introspection that did not align with the narrative I had been clutching in my chest for so long.

Revenge was simple. It was righteous or so I had told myself. However, now in the quiet aftermath, as the satisfaction of darkness of revenge dispelled, something different crawled out.

It happened unexpectedly and unsummoned, the recollection of a past life reached the top of my awareness. A life that felt like it now belonged to someone else entirely.

I leaned my head back onto the cold pillow, closed my eyes, and memories flooded through. A warm day on the beach by the Maid of the Loch, one of those rare Scottish summers when the sun shone like it had been stolen from another country.

We were all huddled together on a beach towel, on the sand and pebbles. I could have heard the sound of their laughter so crisp and clear as if I was back there. The cold water from the shoreline would spray up my legs as the tide would come in, causing my Mum to laugh as the water would soak me.

Her smile was settled as a permanent booking in the mind, the way her eyes contracted at the corners, the sound of her laughter, as if the world was a private affair between the two of us even in those fleeting instances. Memories were vivid, specific in their detail, and therefore more painful for that reason. They weren't just a reminder of what I'd lost they were a reminder of what I could never reclaim. From the very earliest I can remember, I knew I was adopted.

My Mum and Dad had never hidden it from me. I could still visualise the situation when Mum placed me on my seat, her hands soft but strong on my shoulders while she tried to explain in words too deep for me to grasp fully at that moment.

"We chose you," she'd said, her voice steady and warm. "From the moment we saw you, we loved you. Family isn't about blood, sweetheart. It's about love. About standing by each other, no matter what." That love had been unwavering. Mum and Dad had provided me with a welcome and stable home, a family, and the feeling of place that I had completely taken for granted for way too long. I was the youngest of three, James and Amy.

James had been my anchor, solid and steady, a presence as unshakeable as the earth beneath my feet. He wasn't loud or brash, but his quiet strength spoke volumes. Amy was the opposite. Loud, vibrant, and full of life, she had a way of drawing me into her orbit and making me feel like the centre of the universe. Her laughter was infectious, her energy boundless. She never let me to sit on the side lines but inviting me into her world with a determination that made resisting utterly out of question. But even if they adored me, there was always that sense of not belonging which stayed within me. It wasn't them, they loved unconditionally without end, without a doubt.

It was an internal thing, a murmur deep inside my head that I couldn't dismiss. Who was I before they found me? I had put the concept aside many times, tried to ignore it, but it never really left me. It hung around like a ghost, a gap that I couldn't bridge no matter how much they loved me.

As a child the world had felt simpler, safer. Love and family had been enough. But that illusion shattered the night they left me broken and bleeding on the ground, my jaw shattered, my pride torn away. The world revealed itself for what it truly was, merciless, cold, and indifferent. The life I used to live, the life of safety and comfort, belonged to somebody else anymore. It felt like it had been stripped from me, piece by piece, until all that remained was the harsh reality of the path I now walked.

The boy I used to be, felt like a stranger, his laughter and innocence buried under the weight of what I had become.

"You'll be fine," She had painted those words and made me believe there was nothing that could ever really get to me as long as she's around. What would she think if she saw me now? Her son, bruised and bloody, hiding away in a lifeless flat, his hands stained with the blood of men he had hunted down in cold, calculated vengeance. She would have wished for me, in the most absolute sense, only safety, a life free of pain and darkness.

But that life was gone. I was in that darkness, with no way out, not yet anyway. I pulled my duvet tighter and tighter on my body, hoping it would keep the cold out of the flat. The wretchedly harsh early morning unfolded, I went to the window, but I could not see the empty street, nor the slow ascent of the sun. My mind was elsewhere, caught in the endless churn of memory and regret.

The boy I used to be had vanished, swallowed whole by the blackness of the world that is mine. Yet in the stillness of the flat, in the moments when the adrenaline had ebbed and the cold reality of my choices settled in, I couldn't help but wonder if my Mum saw me now, would she even recognise me? Would she ever meet the young man she had known and comforted, whose head she had held in her hands and depended on for comfort?

I then remembered my father with that steady cycle and the peaceful strength. He had never been one for grand gestures or many words. His heart was in the units of activity, like the way he repaired my bike when the chain broke, or in teaching me how to swim. When I was older, it was the simple act of sitting beside me in silence during the moments that didn't need words, his presence enough to steady me. He was my constant, my anchor.

And now, I had cut myself adrift.

I could almost hear his voice in my head, calm and steady, asking the questions I didn't want to answer. What are you doing, son? Is this who you want to be? But he wasn't here to ask those questions. None of them were. I had left them behind. Walked away from their love and the safety they had offered because I couldn't let them see what I had become. I could not make them see the stain of my fists.

James came to mind next. My older brother, always the quiet one, but his silences spoke volumes. He had always been my foundation out of the family, unmoved even during the hardest of days. I could still clearly imagine him standing opposite me, gaze steady, countenance serene but carrying with it the burden of an unspoken question. He wouldn't yell or accuse. He never had. James was the kind of guy who could just look at you and say why, give you the burden of your decision without saying a word.

And Amy... Amy had been my light. Her laughter was what I remembered most. Light and jolly, it had the power to fill up the space of the room, to lift away the bleakness, as if the sunshine penetrated the storm clouds. She possessed this strange quality of pulling me out of the worst parts of myself, her exuberance was so expansive and contagious that it was unimaginable not to feel angry or sad in her presence. She never made me miss out, never made me flinch back too far with myself. Amy used to be quite good at pulling me in with her gravitational centre, drawing me in and making me feel like the point of her universe.

However, that extinguished glow on that night. The following morning, lying bleeding and hopeless on the cold floor, they had not only taken my dignity or my body's ability to resist, but. They had stolen the joy which Amy's laughter had previously brought to my life. They'd swapped it for something cold and hard a shadow which had assimilated me completely. The images of her smile, of her voice, of her laughter were vanishing, worn away by bitterness and loss that had become the new reality.

I have imagined them all whilst staring out the window, gazing down between the roofs of Alexandria.

Mum, Dad, James, Amy. They were there, somewhere, living their lives, untouched by the taint that had now enslaved mine. And I was glad for that. It was better this way. It is better that they remembered me as I had been indeed, and not as the stiff, shattered figure that I now embodied. I didn't know if I will ever see them again. I didn't know if I could. However, the notion that they would discover me as I am now. that was unthinkable.

I closed my eyes and experienced the flat's silence envelope me. They had given me everything. Love. Family. A place to belong. And I had repaid them by walking away. By choosing a path they could never understand, a path that would have horrified them if they knew. I told myself it was for the best. That they were safer this way. Because they didn't have to know that I had been deceitful, nor that the monster I had developed, had become real. But the excuses rang hollow. Deep down, I knew I wasn't just losing them. I was losing something more, a part of myself I would never get back.

None, not even vengeance in the form of the most nature and scale, could ever compensate for what they had extracted from us. I was no longer the child they had adopted into the family, the boy who would call them Mum and Dad. In his place stood someone colder, harder, shaped by anger and pain. I stood up and looked at the pale grey light that came through the blinds. I brought to bear on the weight of finality on my own head, a burden I will never be relieved of. This was who I was now. There was no going back. And yet, in the quiet moments, as the adrenaline faded and the emptiness grew heavier, a question lingered in the back of my mind a question I couldn't ignore, no matter how much I tried. Was this all there was? Was vengeance the only thing left for me? The idea for a second just touched the surface but I pushed it away, flung it deep underneath the sterilising rock of hard emotional resolve which has brought me to this point.

There were still debts to be paid. A price to be exacted in blood. The shadows were my home now. As the brighten of the early morning light brightened, I pulled the blind and drawn the curtain over them, cloaking the day. Once again, I retreated into the darkness.

Dumbarton's Streets

I stepped off the bus onto Dumbarton's High Street, the felt air damp and heavy, with the weight of an impending rainstorm. The low, sombre clouds draped the roofs and cast the town in an oppressive, grey twilight that leached the joy from all they speared.

The cracked pavement and battered shopfronts appeared even more worn than I remembered, as though they too were straining under the same weight as the people who hurried along the street. Most of the shops lining the High Street had long since passed their prime. The paint on their facades was chipped and peeling, their signs cracked or faded to dull shadows of what they once proclaimed. Posters showing curling on windows advertised the same sale, the one that made it feel more desperate than could be made a chance sale. It felt like the whole street teetered on the edge of a fine balancing act between survival and decay, with the odds tipped heavily toward the latter.

The people matched the street, their faces creased with weariness, their steps quick and purposeful as though to linger too long might let the grey settle into their bones. They moved with a quiet urgency, heads down, avoiding eye contact, navigating the cracked pavement like ghosts trying to outrun the slow collapse of the town around them. Mick had sent me here on an errand.

He'd called it a "Simple delivery, " but in Mick's world, nothing was ever simple. Any task that he set upon had behind it, a kind of unsaid burden, a subdermal dome of heavy mystery, under which the meaning lay concealed, and you knew better to ask what it was. This was a test, like all the others, a chance for Mick to measure me against the unyielding standards of his world. He wasn't looking for trust, exactly. Mick didn't believe in trust. What he valued was dependability. He wanted to know that when he handed you a task, you would carry it out without question, without complication. Failure wasn't an option. The package lying in my hand was tidy, in simple brown paper, and secured with robust twine.

It felt unrealistically light and almost weightless, which actually gave it the feeling of the most apparent evil. Anything that was in there was meaningful enough for Mick to put his dependency on me. Deliver it to the address. Keep your head down. Don't draw attention. Simple words, with heavy consequences if you didn't follow through.

I shifted the angle of my grip on the forecasted package, fixed my coat more snugly, as if against the damp air chilling and focused down the High Street, with a point in mind. To the left, a pawn shop lay obscured by dust, its cluttered cases of display suggesting desperation and abandoned dreams and not bargain. Across the way, a failed neon sign, attached to the side of a fish and chips shop, blinked weakly, and the unpleasant smell of stale oil and vinegar spilled out onto the street. Across from it, a bookmaker's stood with its windows plastered in faded posters advertising greyhound races and football matches.

These were the places where Mick's world thrived. In the crevices and dark corners, where nobody asked the questions, where everybody looked away. Behind the decay of peeling paint and flickering signs, there was a rhythm, a pulse of debts and deals, survival, and silence. I walked with my head down, my speed keeping pace with the flow. It wasn't crowded, but there were enough people present that made me feel vulnerable. Every glance in my direction felt weighted, every shift of movement around me seemed to carry some hidden intent. That was the nature of Mick's world. It made you cautious, paranoid. It taught you to question everything, to trust no one.

The address Mick had provided me was at the very edge of the High Street, a corner shop that had the appearance of ready to give way under the pressure of its own neglect. The sign displayed on the door shifted a little in the wind, its tattered lettering hardly discernible beneath the grime. Paint on the shopfront was tenacious, coming away in stubborn stains, and the glass was covered in a layer of grime so high, that it was impossible to figure out what was beyond it. I opened the door, and the clang of the bell above deafening above the dampness of the street.

Moving inward, the shop was a small and squeezed space with cluttered shelves piled high with cans, sweets, and cleaning bottles. A haphazard row of off brand alcohol sat toward the back, their labels faded and peeling, promising nothing but regret for anyone desperate enough to buy them. The heavy overhead lamps hummed weakly, casting harsh, fluorescent light that served only to bring out the dust everywhere. Behind the counter stood an older man, his leathery skin etched with deep lines and his grey hair pulled back into a low ponytail. His hands rested on the counter large, rough, and scarred, the kind of hands that spoke of a lifetime spent working of hard graft, a tough paper round as we say.

His keen eyes rose as I came through the door, and his dark eyes making contact with mine, with a flash of recognition. He didn't speak, just made a small nod to me. It was gentle, that is, the sort of movement that wouldn't be picked up by a stranger in this environment, yet it was significant. Holding the package tighter and tighter, I moved gradually and in a single line toward the counter.

Mick's world demanded patience and precision. It wasn't enough to simply deliver a package. Every action, every word, was a statement a demonstration of whether you could handle the unspoken rules of the life Mick demanded. The man reached out, his actions calm and deliberate. I placed the package on the counter and for a second his gaze and my hand, almost meet. Space around the two of us hummed with a feeling of something deeply understood in the absence of words. "From Mick," I explained, whispering, not too loud but loud enough to be heard by anyone that may be in the shop. The man, at that moment, again nodding his head, reaching out with a tightening grip lifted the package and pulling it towards himself. With a smooth movement, he shoved it under the counter and his face hid his emotions. But his astute eyes kept fixed on me, examining me, analysing me as if he could pierce through the surface to read the anger and devotion which had led me to his door.

When I turned to leave, my attention focused on the door. The package was delivered, the errand complete. That should have been the end of it. However, as soon as my hand reached the cold surface of the door handle, a shout came from behind me, clear and cutting through the silence, that involuntarily froze me in place.

"Oi, Jamie!"

"I Thought I recognised that face." My hand froze on the door, the chill of the metal handle biting into my palm. It was irrefutably that voice, with a disgusting undercurrent of casual triumph that galvanised my stomach in knots. Slowly I turned, the beat of my heart echoing in my ears as I surveyed the dark room of the shop. The figure appeared from the gloom at the back, his thick boots clicking on the ancient floorboards in a calculated beat. I recognised him instantly. The years hadn't done much to change him the same wiry build, the same predatory grin that didn't quite reach his eyes. He was small town also, the kind of guy that lived off of intimidation and meanness. The type who saw power as something you stole from those weaker than you, and who measured his worth in the fear he could elicit.

"Well, well, well" he croaked, adding to the smirk widening on his face as he closed the distance between us, sizing me up, his stare examined me, measuring me, as an animal does it that is about to be sprung, as it is about to be attacked.

"Look who it is. Thought you'd crawled under a rock somewhere. Looks like you couldn't stay out of trouble." The sound of his voice hit me like a blow, stirring memories I'd tried to bury. His sneering face flashed in my mind, a warped reflection of that night, the night they'd broken me, left me bleeding and humiliated. The smirk he wore now was the same one I remembered from back then, the same smug arrogance that made my blood run hot. I made myself inhale steadily, my fingertips flexing in my sides as I looked at him. Mick's world asked for control and losing mine, here and now would cost me more than my vain glory.

"Just passing through," I stated coolly, and I let my voice remain serene and rhythmical, while all within my body screamed to unleash violence. He laughed, a deep, grating, resonant chuckle that echoed through the cramped shop.

"Passing through, eh? Funny. You still rocking that broken jaw out here," he said, ducking his head and grinning wider and wider as he moved closer and closer to me.

"Guess you have at last got out from underneath that rock." The taunt was meant to provoke, to remind me of what they'd done.

My fists resounded at the sides, but I kept them still. The guy at behind the counter moved only a few inches, but looked at us both back and forth, watchful, yet speaking nothing at all. I squared my shoulders, locking eyes with this fucking thug.

"Perhaps I enjoy trouble," I replied, as a glint of my own anger seeped into my tone. For a moment, his smirk faltered. His pupils contracted slightly, and I could sense the building doubt. He was sizing me up, reassessing, trying to reconcile the person standing before him with the one he remembered.

"You've got a mouth on you," he muttered, his tone quieter now, though the bravado was still there, clinging like a bad habit. Before he could say more, the man behind the counter coughed, a sharp, deliberate sound that cut through the tension like a blade.

"That's enough, from you both," the shopkeeper said, his voice calm but carrying an undeniable authority. His gaze fixed on the thug, steady and unyielding.

"You're done here. Keep it up and the police will be called" The shopkeeper paused, taking a shot at a guy who stood in front of me, as the scowl of the guy tightened while the shopkeeper's eyes flickered back and forth between me and this low life thug. For a moment, I thought he might ignore the warning, that he'd push things further out of sheer spite. But his shoulders slumped, and he grunted under his breath a pathetic defiance as he turned and left the shop. With a weak chime. the bell over the door jingled as it slammed shut behind him, and the sound reverberated in the stillness that remained afterwards.

I exhaled slowly, and the tightness went away from my shoulders as I relaxed my fists. Fury still bubbled under the surface, seething and unstoppable, but I pushed it down, deep within. The shopkeeper's voice broke the silence.

"Good," he said, speaking quietly, but with a note of praise.

"You've got control. Micks got an eye for that." I nodded, meeting his gaze. He was right Mick valued control above all else. In his universe recklessness was more than a mistake, but also a risk. To lose your temper meant losing everything, and Mick would never accept defeat.

I remained silent and retraced my steps to the street. The air feels a hell of a lot colder, and the frost is scratching at my skin at every exhalation as I pull my coat tight around me. The High Street was the same oppressive grey, windswept, weather battered as it was, the atmosphere waiting on the very edge of a downpour. I faded into the narrow streets and the current of bodies engulfed me. My mind, however, was elsewhere. The voice of the thug, with his obnoxious laughter, still echoed in my head, the mockery and the smirk repeating themselves like an old record. He'd looked at me like I was still the same person I'd been back then the kid they'd beaten and humiliated. But he didn't get it. That kid was gone. In his place stood someone else entirely. Someone darker, harder. I won't be afraid to show him what I've achieved.

The job was done, the package was sent, but my mind kept replaying the encounter in the shop. It wasn't just about proving myself to Mick anymore. It was about proving something to myself. Each time I did these fucking tests, I experienced a small change in myself, my confidence grew each time and felt like I became a changed person, a person tinged with anger, with grief, with resentment and a desire for retribution, reborn in my search for revenge, no longer broken and weak. I was so deep into Mick's world now and would I be ready for whatever he threw at me next.

Into Rosshead

The Heavy air carried an eerily quiet tension as I walked into Rosshead, a place where even the wind seemed to hesitate, unsure whether it should disturb the silence. Rosshead wasn't a place people simply visited unless they had a reason to. Every corner, every narrow lane carried its own brand of quiet hostility, the kind that lingered long after footsteps faded. The estate was a mix of tired council flats and semidetached houses, where small attempts to brighten the monotony, a freshly painted fence, a cluster of potted plants placed by a door were unnoticeable by the relentless bleakness of the place. The streets bore a heavy, weary silence, broken only by the occasional distant shout or the low rumble of a passing car.

This wasn't a scheme for outsiders. You kept your head down, stayed in your lane. I walked down through Halkett Crescent with my hood covering my face, shrugging my shoulders tight from the chill. My movements were instinctive, the way anyone learned to carry themselves here if they wanted to avoid attention. Blend in. Become part of the grey. Just another shadow among many.

The flats adjacent to me towered over me in a quite indifferent way, their damaged exteriors riddled with imprints of neglect and dirt over time. The flats may have lived, in the past, with a peppered finish, but the erosion of the bow had left them bare now. Broken glass littered the uneven pavements, mingling with the soggy remains of takeaway wrappers. Even the weeds that pushed through the cracks in the concrete seemed to cling to life with a kind of stubborn defiance, growing where nothing else dared.

From fairly close by I made out the soft drone of a train rattling along the rails from Balloch to Alexandria and then on to Glasgow. The sound was muted, almost dreamlike, a reminder that life moved on just beyond the confines of these streets. But not for me. Rosshead was a place you didn't just walk through. It swallowed you whole, left you feeling marked. I sank deeper and deeper into the labyrinthine streets, past towering multi-level buildings in a silent, dark streetwise strip.

Graffiti plastered the walls, claimed by stakes of local gangs which seemed long gone, I mean who the fuck are the Rosshead Posse anyway, but their ghost still lingers in the minds of the people who experienced places like this. From the windows of the flats, the shades were drawn down, but I could still tell that there lurked unseen eyes that were keeping tabs on me. Flickers of motion caught my attention, the odd curtain twitching, a shadow slipping behind the glass. Nobody wanted to be seen, but everyone wanted to know who was in the street. They wouldn't dare get involved, but they wouldn't forget either.

I made my way toward Colquhoun Drive and found a spot to sit, half hidden in the shadow of a towering council block. The cold concrete pressing, seeping inwards towards my back as I settled in, letting the darkness swallow me. Sitting from this position, I could see the street unseen. Time passed slowly, the hours stretching out as the chill of the air seeped into my bones. My jaw ached a constant, familiar throb and the scars on my knuckles felt tight in the biting cold. The pain felt solid, a constant cue of why I was being brought here. Each scar, each ache carried a name, and tonight I was one step closer to crossing another off the list.

The sky turned a washed plum as the last of the light from the day receded. Around me, the estate began to stir. Doors swung open and shut, and children poured into the streets laughing, shouting, and echoing all the while. A few kicked a battered football back and forth across the cracked pavement, their voices echoing through the alleys. At the edge of the railway track, a gang of teenagers stood in the corner of the little football field. Hoodies pulled up, hands buried in their pockets, they moved with the languid caution of those who'd grown up too fast, their actions deliberate and guarded. One of them turned toward me, nodding in silent acknowledgment a gesture that meant everything and nothing in a place like this. We didn't know each other, but here, a nod was enough.

The train rolled by one more time, this time its sound much louder, a temporary break in the quiet. I saw its lights disappear into the distance and for a brief moment I questioned myself what it might be like to board that train and go. Leave Alexandria. Leave everything behind. The thought came and went, fleeting and impossible. Escape wasn't for people like me. Patience had to become second nature to me, I learned the hard way. Mick had been drilled into me over weeks, months it wasn't waiting. It was about timing, about knowing when everything was aligned just right.

Streetlamps began to turn on, producing a weak, jaundiced light on the damaged asphalt. It continued to get colder and unforgiving, however I remained fixed my spot, my breath turning to fog. And then I saw him. He came out of a maisonette block on Colquhoun Drive, a silhouette in shadow against the feeble light emanating from the doorway. I recognised him instantly, Ross Campbell despite the years. Time had mellowed them out, mellowed them all, in ways that they did not perceive. He was fatter now, the size of his belly pushing against the seams of the sweatshirt. His face was gaunt, his eyes hollow, but there was still a sharpness to his features a twitchy wariness that told me he hadn't completely lost the edge that made him dangerous.

He stood there for a moment, scanning the street with a lazy gaze that didn't match the tension in his posture. He moved like someone who'd spent too many years looking over his shoulder, and I wondered if he'd felt it, some creeping awareness that his past was coming for him. I moved out of the darkness, observing from a safe distance as he began to move. His pace was slow, purposeful, and the slap of his boots on the gravel a faint but reliable sound. I followed, staying far enough back to remain unseen. He made a right turn onto Halkett Crescent, then a left turn onto Heather Avenue, I was forcing myself to get less lively with each stride.

The cold air bit through my hoodie but I ignored it. My focus was on him, on the way he carried himself. He didn't know yet. But he would. A low — lit streetlight illuminated over him as he came to a halt by a neighbour's wall. He stood there for a moment, his head tilting slightly, as though he'd heard something. I froze, tucking myself behind a bush, holding my breath, barely holding him in my sight as he glanced over his shoulder. He stood there for a moment, motionless, his body contorted, his gaze roaming the blackness. Then, slowly, he relaxed, shaking his head.

That was his biggest mistake. I moved quicker, trying to reduce the sound my boots make crunching against the gravel. His head snapped around, his eyes widening in recognition.

"Alright dickface, Remember me?" I said through gritted teeth, my voice low and growling. Ross's eyes swept wildly, each breath on his chest hitching in panicked breaths he backed up while an attempt made its way to create a distance between us. It wasn't fear at first no, it was confusion, the kind of unease that flickers just beneath the surface before the full weight of understanding crashes down. But I could see the moment it hit him. His face went pale, his breath hitching as recognition settled in.

"The fuck do you want," a whisper, the words barely audible. His voice was breathy, unsteady, the confidence he used to wear now breaking down under the weight of truth. I moved closer, the bat held against my shoulder, solid and reassuringly heavy. My grip tightened around the handle, the rough wood pressing into my palm like an extension of myself.

"Surprised to see me?" I asked, my tone low, the question sharp enough to cut through the cold night air. His hands rose unconsciously, palms open in a feeble attempt to push me away.

"Wait hold on," he stammered, his voice rising in pitch as panic took hold.

"I don't... I don't know what you think."

"What the fuck do you mean, you don't know?" I snapped, closing the gap between us in one deliberate step. The bat swung down without warning, and the dull, meaty thud of wood meeting flesh and bone echoed in the stillness. The blow hit him in the ribs and blew him air from his lungs in a gasped cry. He fell to his knees, one hand on the ground the other gripping his side, he strained in pain.

"Jesus fucking Christ!" he wheezed, doubling over as he tried to steady himself. I didn't wait for him to recover. The bat fell down again, and stronger this time, hitting the back of his legs. His knee buckled, and he hit the ground with a grunt, the gravel scraping against his palms as he tried to catch himself.

"Now do you remember." I growled, my voice deep, commanding.

"Please," he yelled, words spilling out in a rush of panicked speech.

"I... I don't even know what this is about! I didn't do anything!"

"Didn't do anything?" The laugh that escaped me was cold, hollow, devoid of any real amusement.

"You didn't do anything when you held me down?"

"When the lot of you beat me up while laughing, breaking my jaw to pieces, and dropping me on the floor, to bleed out? That wasn't you?"

His mouth opened, and shut again, and his words become present in his closed larynx. He shook his head with little strength, his whole body shaking in the process as he leaned backward on hands and knees.

"I didn't... I didn't... I wasn't..." I stopped him with another swing, the bat connecting him across the shoulder with a sickening sound. He cried out, a sound unrefined and visceral, as he now crumpled onto his side.

"Don't fucking lie to me," I snarled, stepping over him.

"You remember exactly what you did." The cold night air stung my skin, but the fire burning in my chest drowning it out.

"I swear," he croaked, his voice barely audible. He desperately tried to push himself up, but his arms buckled beneath him, and he fell back to the ground,

"I didn't have a choice!" coughing and gasping for air.

"Not personal? No Choice?" The words dripped with disbelief and fury. I bent over to him, taking hold of a fist full of his hoodie and lifting him.

"You think that makes it better? That you were just following orders?" His gaze struck mine, round and terrified, overflowing wet with unseen tears.

"Please," he whispered, his voice breaking.

"I'm sorry. I... I didn't mean for any of it to happen." The apology was too late, too hollow. I threw him hard against the solid ground, the force jarring through his frame and another pained cry got trapped in his very chest.

"You didn't mean for it to happen? I hissed, my voice low and steady.

"You meant every fucking second of it. You enjoyed it. I saw it in your face, in your smile, in the way you once looked at me as if I was nothing." His lips shook, while his whole body shook uncontrollably as he fixed his gaze upon me, his countenance pale, dusted with soil and blood. I stood over him, the bat hanging loosely in my hand, its weight a comforting presence. For a split second, I ended up accepting, the silence, with his noisy, irregular breaths and the soft whisper of the breeze in the neighbouring trees.

"You thought there would be no retaliation, that I was some weak cunt" I said finally, my tone cold and measured.

"You thought I'd just vanish off the face of the earth, you'd never have to see what you'd done." Snapping at him, he shook his head, his movements weak and jerky.

"I didn't... I thought you were dead, you know," he confessed, in a voice no louder than a flea in a frying pan. The phrases sent a new surge of rage through my body, a stabbing and burning pain.

"You left me for dead, that much is true" I spat, raising the bat again.

"But I survived. And now, I'm going to make sure you never forget that."

Ross tried to scuttle backward, his hands scraping at the gravel as he attempted to put some distance between us. His breath came in short, panicked gasps, punctuated by pained groans every time his battered body shifted. Crouching, I held the bat up, comfortable feeling as I moved towards him.

"You don't get to crawl away," I said, my voice cold and steady.

"Not after everything you did."

"Please," he gaffed, afraid, his sound barely more than a croak.

"I'll do anything, just... just, stop!"

"Stop?" I tilted my head, studying him like he was some pathetic creature I'd found writhing in the dirt.

"Did you stop when I begged? When I was bleeding and broken, did you stop?" He didn't answer, couldn't answer. His lips trembled and his eyes darted wildly in search of an exit, a miracle, but which wasn't appearing. I moved then one step in the direction, a swinging violent impact smashing the bat on the gravel next to his skull. The force impact caused stones to roll across his face and he instinctively threw back a choked cry.

"Now look at me," I said, my voice cutting through the chill of the night. dirt smeared across his cheeks, blood trickling from his nose and the corner of his mouth, his expression twisted with a mix of terror and pain.

"You think you can just walk away from what you did?" I hissed, crouching down so our faces were level.

"Do you really think you are gonna keep on living your life as nothing happened while I'm stuck with scars you inflicted on me?" He shook his head weakly, his breaths hitching as he tried to form words.

"I... I didn't know...," Ross murmuring again, my patience all but gone with his bullshit now

"Stop saying you didn't know?" My voice rose, the anger bubbling to the surface in a sharp, bitter laugh.

"You didn't know what? That it would leave me broken? That it would haunt me every damn day?" I got a hold of him by the neck, pulling him towards me with a violent force that produced a new surge of pain through his body. He let out a pained grunt, his hands clawing weakly at mine in a futile attempt to loosen my grip.

"You're pathetic," I spat, my voice dripping with contempt. Every ounce of that power and control you thought you had. Look at you now.

"You're nothing." I snapped, His eyeballs welled with tears, his whole body shook in my arms as I trapped him there, making him confront the whole force of my rage.

"I'm sorry," he whispered, the words shaky and broken.

"I'm sorry, I swear."

"Sorry is not enough," I murmured, angrily.

"You don't get to use a worthless apology. You can't just erase what you did to me with a couple of words." I shoved him back down, his body hitting the ground with a heavy thud. He groaned, clutching his side where the bat had cracked against his ribs earlier.

"You think you're in pain now? I asked, my tone cold and detached.

"You don't even know the meaning of the word." I held the bat up once more, taking it in both hands, standing above him. He witnessed the movement and made a weak effort to protect himself by raising his hands, but it was all in vain. The bat hit with a sickening crack to his forearm. His scream tore through the night, raw and guttural, a sound that sent a strange mix of satisfaction and disgust coursing through me.

"Hurts, doesn't it? I said, my voice steady despite the storm raging inside me.

"That's just a taste of what you gave me. Of what you left me to deal with while you carried on like nothing happened." He was sobbing now, pathetic, choked sobs escaping his lips as he held up his arm.

"Please," he gasped, his voice barely audible.

"I can't... I can't take it..." I crouched beside him, the bat resting across my knees. My voice dropped to a low, even tone, cold as the night air around us.

"You don't get to decide when it ends. You gave up that right the moment you decided I wasn't worth more than a laugh." He fixed his gaze upon me, a pale countenance with streaks of tears, blood trickling ceaselessly to the gravel at his feet. His lips moved, words took shape, but nothing occurred.

"Here's what's going to happen," I said, my voice calm and deliberate.

"You're going to remember this night. Each time you see your arm, each time you take a step, feel the pain in your ribs, you will have a memory of what you did. And you'll remember me." I straightened, holding the bat securely as I retreated. He slumped against the ground, his body trembling as he let out a weak, shuddering sob.

"For a time, you shall survive," I explained, my voice echoing his pained sounds.

"If I do ever see you again, if I even hear your name, you won't be able to walk away next time." He didn't respond, maybe couldn't respond. He just sat there, shattered, defeated, a flurry of sobs muffling to the silence of night. Turning, I walked away, the bat dangling with ease naturally at my side. My steps were slow, deliberate, the crunch of gravel beneath my boots the only sound as I disappeared over the tin bridge and into the darkness. I left him as he did me, a broken victim, coughing, wheezing, his body fighting and burning from the brutal assault. But I didn't look back.

In The Shadows

I trudged along the deserted streets of Tullichewan, the air was damp and clinging, as if the night itself refused to let go of me. My breath hung in pale clouds, briefly visible before disappearing into the dark. My hands stayed jammed deep inside my jacket pockets trying to keep any sort of heat, although they pulsed in pain, a steady reminder of what has happened these past few weeks. The fight was over for now, but the echoes lingered in my bones, the adrenaline leeching away in slow, dragging waves, leaving behind an unsettling mix of emptiness and a hollow, fleeting satisfaction.

The streets were still, the schemes silences in Tullichewan were soothing to me. They also had a fragile, unsettled feel about them, punctuated by the detached bark of a dog in the distance or the haunted whine of a siren rushing down the A82. Some streetlights still burned, their weak light pulsating faintly above cracked roads. Slender, deep shadows concentrated in every recess, big and threatening, as if the void, the black, could tell what happened recently.

Having pain throughout my fingers, a low hum began in my first knuckles, progressed through my radius and ulna. Every blow would sink deep into my body, blazing in my mind's eye. I could still feel the resistance of his body under my palms, the pricking pain of bone on flesh, how his face had contorted from a smug look of indifference to pure, unfiltered horror. Struck by that flash of realisation, understanding who I was and why I was there it had roused a hidden feeling deep within me, a feeling of pure, primal instinct.

Yet as I moved from the scene, that fire inside also began to cool, its embers dropping to ash. The euphoric feeling of satisfaction was only there a moment, fleeting and heady, as it was vanishing from out of reach, leaving me again with that visceral sensation of emptiness, the one that plagued me always. His face the blood, the swelling, the terror remained in me, not due to his culpability nor regret but because his action didn't suffice. But the emptiness within me still stretched on evermore, a huge, unassailable, dark cave which I could not, no matter how many blows I struck, no matter how much terror I caught in my reflection, fill. Beneath the dim, flickering streetlights, I felt more alone than ever. The kicking should have been enough. The fear I'd seen in him should have validated everything. However, as I walked along the streets in the cold, deserted environment, the familiar pain resonated in a deeper, argumentative tone.

By the time I reached the flat, my thoughts were a tangled mess of static, an unrelenting noise that wouldn't quiet. The pungent smell of cigarette smoke hit me in the face as I opened the door, mixing with the old odour in the room. Paul was waiting for me. He lounged in his usual spot, slouched back in his chair with one foot propped on the edge of the table. His cigarette was almost gone, with the tip smoking down near the bottom in the soft light of the shadows in the corner of the room. He lifted his head and then I walked in, and his sharp eyes glinting met my hand, intensely. Biographical, little bows of blood on my knuckles showed him everything he wanted to see.

He remained speechless for a while, only looking at me, his countenance impassive. At last, he spoke, his voice a rumbling, echoing groan, a barren cavern scraping on smooth stone.

"Didn't think you'd go that deep," he said, though there was no judgment in his tone just a quiet wariness. I shrugged, leaning against the kitchen counter. There it was the cold surface pressing against my lower back as I watched out the window. My image mirrored back at me, blunted by the veined window glass and the void of the streetlight exterior. The shadowy outline of a man I barely recognised.

"Things got messy," I said. My voice was expressionless, artificial even to my own ears. Paul exhaled through his nose, a sharp, irritated sound. He stubbed out his cigarette in the overflowing ashtray with quick, almost violent motions, as if he were trying to crush more than just the smoke.

"Aye," he muttered, his voice heavy with meaning.

"But you're takin' it personal, brother. I've said it before don't let it find its way into your head. You keep doing it this way, it's gonna kill you eventually."

"Maybe it already has." The sentences came out quietly before I could stop them, minty and sour. Paul's pupils constricted, having the crystalline sting, but he did not flinch. Rather, he got up and walked to the cupboard, reaching in, and taking out two glasses. He topped each with whisky and the amber glow within it flickered in the failing light before he slid one across to the table to me. I did it, not in the hope of getting it, but in reaction to the need for anything to blunt the keen cutting edge of the cold that had taken hold low in my body.

Its first taste burned my throat, a flaming current that ended in a clinical, inexplicable heat that, for one reason or another, craved to close the ragged ends of the will to capitulate. The liquid, golden and bright, carried an almost medicinal sharpness that bit back as it settled. A smoky drapery rose and descended, leaving a peaty, even animalistic aroma on my nose, a scent of wooden barrels, of burnt wood.

I let the next sip linger on my tongue. It was fuller this time, dredging up previously obscured beams beneath the primary roast honeyed sweetness overlaid with the subtlest tang of orange peel, as if waving a mistaken balm that never quite came through. It lingered on the palate, a slow, soothing current of warmth against the storm of my mind, which failed in its mission of calming the turmoil that stirred within me. Standing in front of the table, Paul swirled the scotch in his glass.

He fixed me with his gaze, his tone softer now, even almost hesitant. He was weighing each word carefully.

"I know you're after something more than just a punch up with some scumbags. Yet, you should think about what is being lost."

I stayed silent, my fingers tightening around the glass.

"Every punch, every hit," Paul continued, his voice low and steady,

"It's a piece of yourself you're leaving behind. And for what? These blokes they're not worth it. None of them are worth losing yourself over." His words cut deeper than I wanted to admit.

For a few moments maybe more, they pierced the whisky haze and fury, penetrating the bare, open, true self of I which I have long ago tried to hide. My mind drifted, unbidden, to my family. Mum, Dad, James, and Amy back home, living in the world I had walked away from. They pictured in their mind's eye, looking out for them, I was living miles away, making a name to be proud of. But if they knew the truth, if they could just see me now. Mum's voice came to me then, soft but steady, as if she were standing right there in the room.

"You're better than this," she'd said to me once, after I'd come home bloodied and bruised from a fight at school.

"You're better than what the world thinks you are." I'd believed her back then, clung to her words like a lifeline.

But standing there in that grimy, smoky flat with my own bloody palm print and a cocktail of scotch in my hand, I felt uncertain no more. The one she'd trusted, the one she'd taught, was not the boy she raised, one I scarcely recognised. Paul's voice broke me out of a state.

"There are people who care for you." he said, his voice firm.

"Good people. If they knew what you were up to, they'd be worried sick. don't let this. whatever it really is. Cost your relationship with them too."

I didn't respond. What could I say? He was right, but it didn't matter. I had made my choice. Paul didn't try to stop me when I left the flat. He didn't have to. We both knew there wasn't anything left to say. The door slammed shut behind me, the noise somehow final, as if it has closed the past life from the present life, the past me, from the present me.

The streets outside were as cold and empty as when I'd arrived. A low hum of the streetlamps vibrated faintly overhead and cast pools of desaturated yellow that barely spanned to the broken pavement. The breath fogged under the cold air, escaping into the night, and then with dissipation into the inky blackness. I walked aimlessly, since the cold wind bit my cheeks, the buildings stood quiet and in shadow. Streets lay deserted with the possible exception of the sounds of brittle leaves skittering across the ground in the wind. Everything felt heavy the air, the silence, the weight of Paul's words hanging over me like a shroud. 'Every punch, every hit, it's a piece of yourself you're leaving behind.' playing on repeat in my mind, I plunged my arms further into my pockets and the rough feeling of my jacket against my knuckles caught my attention.

I couldn't argue with Paul. He was, and although I despise the fact that he was right. But I also knew I couldn't stop. The memories had me now. They only appeared in the calm moments, slithering up like spectres at the boundaries of my thought. I remembered mum and her peaceful yet firm hands as she nursed grazed knees when I was a child.

"My blue-eyed boy, you're tougher than you think," she'd say, her voice steady and comforting.

Back then, it had been enough to make me believe her, pick myself up and carryon with the day as if nothing happened. I also pictured Dad, his unassuming power, his ability to make me feel secure without uttering a sound. He wasn't one for long talks or emotional outbursts, but his presence had always been enough. Just knowing he was there had been enough. And James, my big brother. Solid, dependable James. He was my safe harbour, growing up, being quietly, consistently on the lookout out for me. Then there was Amy. Laughter emanated from her like sunshine through a rainy sky, unremitting, and no less ephemeral still. She had this way of making everything feel lighter, even when the weight of the world felt unbearable. I almost heard the rolling of her eyeballs mocking me for overthinking and looping skipping ropes around me like a trap, while tripping me in the corner feeling ashamed. But that was a lifetime ago. A world away from where I stood now, with blood on my hands and a purpose that felt more like a curse. If they could see me now, if they knew what I had become. I shook my head, but I could not get rid of the pictures and the memories invading me like a creeping, penetrating, cold, deep in my bones, clutching, which wouldn't let go. Suddenly I found myself walking back, in my wanderings, to the bottom of Levenvale of all places and the little park by the railway tracks.

It also seemed to be rather empty in the dim light of the street lighting. The swings creaked softly in the wind, the chains rusted and worn. The goalposts stood like skeletal sentinels, their peeling paint barely clinging to the metal. I stood at the brink of the pile and my breath became very shallow as recollections flowed over me. I could imagine it so vividly the ghost of my younger self running across the field, giggling, while James chased after him. I could almost feel the impact of the ball on my foot and the rhythmic applause as it flew past the makeshift goal. Do that, I'd proclaimed, demonstrating to James how to put on a show, how to retain possession of the ball. He'd stared at me with his big eyes, his face glowing with delight while he learned to imitate me. He hadn't been very successful back then, just elbows and knees, but he'd never given up.

The Memory evoked a fleeting smile to my mouth, but it couldn't, alas, stick. It couldn't. That boy was gone. The world he'd known was gone, replaced by something colder, darker, and unrelenting. I slumped down hard on one of the derelict seats by the edge of the playing surface, bringing my body forward by resting my elbows across my knees and my head down into my hands. The cold wood of the bench seeped through my jacket, but I barely felt it. The pain in my chest was excruciating, a hollow, aching pain that wouldn't be left alone. I'd thought revenge would be enough. I'd thought it would give me back some semblance of control, some sense of justice. It can, however, but rather, carve out fresh lesions, more trenchant and ragged than the ones that are afoot to reverse. Every swing of the bat I'd thrown earlier had felt like a release, a way to purge the anger that had been eating away at me for years.

Nevertheless, following stillness, it became clear the animosity was not yet finished. It was still there, simmering just beneath the surface, waiting for the next excuse to rise up and consume me. A train whistle thundered through the quiet of the night, startling me out of my daydreaming. Its beam covered the area, landing on the old rusty swings and unkempt growth for a brief moment, only to be swallowed once more by the night. The shriek of train wheels against rails still hung in the air even after the train had gone. 'Every punch, every hit it's a piece of yourself you're leaving behind.' Was he right? Was I losing pieces of myself every time I struck out, every time I let the anger take over? The question nagged at me, sharp to the bone, but I held no answers, none.

Maybe I didn't want one. I got up, the cold ran over my cheeks, and I plunged my hands back into my pockets. The park stretched out before me, empty and desolate, a stark reminder of everything I'd lost. I cast one last glance at the cracked goal posts, the splintered swings and, with a sigh, turned and walked back to the street. The buildings loomed around me, their dark windows were like empty eyes watching my every move. Streets were surprisingly empty, muffling all sound from the graceful exhale of the wind whistling through the trees as well as the quiet self — discharge of the last havers of the town, a baby put and down no longer to be picked up as long as night continued on its way through the breeze, it longed for its place to be dropped by one or more put down passengers.

I flashed Mum to my mind again, her voice like a soft, yet strong embrace, encasing me like a safety net that shouldn't have been there for me.

"You're better than this," she'd said once, her words filled with a quiet conviction that had made me believe her. But was I? The concept lay heavy upon my chest, its pointiness cutting through to my awareness as I walked. Maybe there was a period when I was a dreamer, a period when I could have stayed away from all of it. But that time was gone, lost to the shadows that now consumed me. But deep down, there was a residual of hope.

A faint, stubborn spark that refused to be extinguished. Maybe one day there will be a way out. Perhaps I could break the cycle before it ruined me entirely. But not yet. There were still debts to be paid, a face to confront, one more person who needed to understand that I wasn't the same boy they'd tried to break. Until that was done, until I'd reclaimed every piece of myself, they'd taken, I couldn't stop. I pulled my hood over the head blasts of wind rising up and I walked on, the streets receding in dark, implacable lines. Shadows were my reality, and I would crawl through them one footstep at a time in search of an escape. For now, that was enough.

Behind the Mask

The heavy grey sky above Alexandria looked threatening to rain, but the grey masses would not part ways. The encroaching shadows moved across the skyline in a slow, rolling tide, enveloping the town in a strangling veil between the valleys of the surrounding hills. The air was stuffy, wetted, and intrusive, lodging in every corner, blotting porous skin and psyche in equal measure.

It wasn't the type of rain that you could prepare for, but a ceaseless, heavy, wetness that fell upon all things, speeding each action, breath, and heartbeat. I walked along the dark and narrow streets, my head tucked low in my shoulders, in an inward struggle against the elements, and against the tumult within my soul. My fingers wedged in tight in my pockets, nails digging into my palms. The sting was clarifying, a welcome distraction from the dredge memories trying to get in. It wasn't just the dampness imprisoned me, but the photograph of him, the final bastard. The very same one who'd been using an iron bar clinically efficaciously, rendering me dismembered and battered in all possible ways. His face haunted me, his features carved into my memory like a cruel spectre.

I may yet 'feel' in the form of cold metal against my teeth, the clean break of bone and the ringing of my own jaw in my head. The previous night had caused deeper trauma than contusions and bone or joint fractures. It had sucked out my core, dehydrated me into a stranger I once was. My jaw hurt at the thought of speaking and at the moment of taking a bite to eat, a perpetual reminder of my malcontents not to retaliate. However, and this is truly worse, was the shame, a quietly intense fire burning from the inside of me. I've had sat on it for months, building up a noxious stew, but tonight, I'd resolved to reclaim what was mine.

Temples tensed, claws retracting towards the surface, I girded for the sensation ahead. Paul had watched it in my gaze the longing, the plan, the burning need for revenge. It didn't matter if he, in fact, gave it out or finished with it. This was my path now. Not even Paul's warnings could sway me. I was just arriving at Paul's flat; a moment of hesitation seized me for a split second. The door loomed before me, its weathered wood scarred by time and countless confrontations. As I pushed it open, it done so without a click, and then an attack of old tobacco and old leather hit me with the force of a brick wall. Beneath it lingered something sharper, metallic, and unnameable a scent that seemed to hang in the corners of his sparce living room.

The flat was bleak, as always. Dim, dusty light seeped in at the grimy windows, producing ragged silhouettes that danced and warped on the floor. Paul sat in his usual spot, the battered armchair by the window. The dim glow framed his angular face, every line and scar a testament to the wars he'd fought. The moment I walked in, his intelligent and piercing look locked gaze with mine. Unbending, rigid, and straight-backed stands Paul, bearing the scars of both ordeal and privation and emerged as a servant hardened not shattered. His knuckles, marked by decades of fights, and the streaks of grey in his hair weren't signs of defeat. They were badges of survival.

"Where you been kid?" Paul asking, a straight to the point, clipped quality the voice of assembled man. The way he looked at me felt like a mirror, a reflection of my own tightly wound intensity. I didn't respond. It was a phantom ambition to keep the feeling of anger from surfacing under me. Paul would just see right through it, and tonight, I didn't care about masks. He gestured to the armchair across from him.

"Sit," he said, the single word a command. Despite the tension coiling in my body, I sat. Once I found myself on its edge the chair let out a groan as I slid down onto it, and I flinched as a side effect.

Paul lit a cigarette, the flame under the match momentarily burning its way into the array of scars that characterised his appearance. He inhaled a full lung, the red glow of the tip pulsating like a heartbeat above him, before releasing a billow of smoke that swirled between them.

"Who's the target? he asked, his tone devoid of surprise or judgment. He wasn't querying whether there was one Paul knew it well enough for that.

"The one who done the most damage, Scars," I, with a definite voice, my jaw involuntarily tightened in response to the swell of anger building in me.

"The one who took the bar to my face." Paul's facial expression became rigid, for a moment a subtle expression of inaudibility appeared on his face. He took another drag from the cigarette, the smoke thickening the air between us.

"The guy who left you bleeding in the house?" Nodding I felt, the memory like acid in my veins. The humiliation, the helplessness it all resurfaced. Paul leaned forward, his elbows resting on his knees.

"There is a distinction between hurting a man and killing him," he said, his voice quiet but firm.

"You'd better decide which one you want."

"Because you can't turn back once you walk a path you aren't prepared for"

His words hit like a gut punch, the weight of them sinking deep into my chest.

"Killing him, hurting him?" I gasped, the query coming out in front of my mouth before I could stop it. Paul's gaze hardened; his eyes boring into mine.

"If you're looking to make him, feel pain, that's one thing. But killing a man? Taking his life and watching his last breath. That changes you. You'll be left a different person and it's not always for the best."

The silence stretched, thick and suffocating. Paul wasn't offering me an out. He projected a mirror and called for me to look into the mirror, while pointing at the transformation I was going through from who I am. I sat frozen, the weight of his words settling over me like a heavy fog. My initial urge was to deflect, to dismiss, a witty retort or a casual chuckle but I could not muster up the courage.

The genuineness in his voice anchored me to the chair, compelling me to stay with the pain it awoke.

"Do you even know why you're doing this?" Paul's voice was steady, deliberate.

"Or is it just about proving to yourself that you're not weak?" My chest constricted, the sentence hitting a nerve, and shouldn't be.

"It isn't about being weak," I mumbled, but as soon as the words left my lips, they seemed empty. Paul recoiled and crossed his arms, while looking at me.

"Then what is it about? Do you really think that this will fix anything in you killing him?" Paul firmly said, I swallowed the words hard, avoiding his gaze. He had a knack of clearing the clutter, peeling away the excuse that I wrapped myself in. I really did not want to be hear this and now, but there was a begrudgingly appreciative part of me that was pleased that he cared enough to make the effort.

"You don't understand," I said, my voice barely audible. "Don't I?" Paul shot back; his tone sharp but kind. "You are not the only one who has walked this road, and you will not be the only one to do so. But let me say, revenge is a tricky business. It doesn't stop where you think it will. It eats at you, little by little, until there's nothing left." I looked down at my hands, which were writhed tight enough that my knuckles were stark white. I wanted to argue, to push back against his words, but I couldn't. The truth was, I didn't know where this path would end, or if I'd even recognise myself when I got there.

Paul leaned forward, his voice softening.

"You need to ask yourself if this is really about him, or if it's about you. Because if you're not careful, you're going to lose more than just your enemy in this fight." His words lingered in the air, heavy and unyielding. I didn't have an answer, or even offer a response or reply. I let the space that separates us thicken between us as a mantle. I questioned whether Paul was right. If this wasn't just about what had been taken from me, but about the pieces of myself I was willing to sacrifice to take control back.

Paul's gaze didn't waver, but his shoulders relaxed slightly as if he'd said all he could. The air between us remained heavy, a strange mix of confrontation and concern. I felt a pang of guilt he hadn't asked for this. He wasn't the one who had to carry this weight, yet here he was, holding part of it anyway.

"Thanks," I mumbled, and the expression became stuck I mouth as it felt out of place. Paul tilted his head slightly, his expression unreadable.

"I'm not telling you what to do," he said.

"You've got to make that call yourself. Yet if you step out of this door, just... don't leave the lessons you learned behind." I forced a small nod, though his words landed like a blow. My throat was constricted, my thoughts a tsunami of conflicting feelings.

Was I even capable of holding onto that part of me? Had I already abandoned my upbringing, piece by piece, with each step and decision I'd made along this road? Paul leaned back, his chair creaking under his weight, and finally looked away. The faint sound of laughter and clinking glasses filtered in from the bar, a cruel reminder of how life went on around us, oblivious to the war raging inside me. I stood, my movements stiff, as though the act of leaving this room and flat required more strength than I had.

My hand lingered on the back of the chair, and for a moment, I considered staying. Perhaps if I just sat here some time could naturally delay what came next. But Paul's eyes found mine again, and this time they held something different a quiet understanding. A small nod, barely perceptible, told me that he wouldn't stop me, wouldn't hold me back. The decision was mine. It always had been.

"Don't give up on yourself," he murmured, his tone becoming gentler now, almost an entreaty. I didn't answer. I didn't trust myself to. All of a sudden, I started to feel like I should turn back and go through that door, that cool night felt like the answer as I moved to the path on the other side of the door. For just a second, I stood frozen, as much as the movement of the street could press on my body. I could still sense the pressure of Paul's sounds; the resonant echo of his voice that told me how much was at risk. But the fire inside me refused to be extinguished. It burned low and steady, guiding my next steps as I pulled my coat tighter and moved into the night.

The wet streets of Alexandria shimmered beneath me, dim and wet, illuminated by the flickering glow of lampposts overhead. The sounds of the town were absent, like they had been absorbed by humidity. My footsteps sounded muffled against the concrete, slow, deliberate. As the bar was now a few streets behind me, the image of his face flitted as a hurried, a blurry recognition, fuelling the intensity of the fire within me.

I pulled my coat tighter on my body, the cold pressure of the heavy atmosphere crawling through my wet clothes and onto my skin. Paul's words played on a loop in my head, a constant undertow beneath my thoughts. There's a fine line between revenge and survival. You'd better know which side you're on. I clenched my fists, the cold, rough surface of the object in my pocket grounding me. It was not the weight of the metal, but the weight of what a power, control, and reclaiming of my stolen peace has come to mean and yet, Paul's voice refused to leave me.

'Breaking him will cost you. Are you ready to pay?' The lane reduced in size as I made the turn on the street, the darkness denser as I walked further in. Walls with their foul and greasy dampness rose up to reach the top. The faint stench of decay mingled with the distant hum of the town's brewery, a strange reminder of the rot that festered, both here and inside me. I stopped, resting my back against the cold brick, my breath visible in the heavy air. The memories surged again, unbidden, and unrelenting. His laughter, sharp and cruel, echoing in the dark. His arms moved with precision, controlled movements, gripping the steel rod like an extension of his own body. The sickening snap of bone, the searing of my jaw that had blasted my voice and left me choking on the floor.

This wasn't about humiliation anymore. It wasn't even about pain. This was about taking back control, about rewriting the narrative he'd forced upon me. My jaw tightened, and the dull throb, a sensitisation to the events from before. I kicked the wall and started to walk again, the rhythm of the town's heartbeat weak and unsteady beneath my shoes. Taking a step towards the next street the pub foreshortened before me, its fluctuating lit sign cast a small form of a silhouette of the pavement.

I stepped across the road and stood against a lamp post gathering my thoughts before entering, the cold metallic sharp click into my back. From here, I could see the entrance clearly, the door swinging open and shut as drunken people drifted in and out. None of them were him, not yet. I looked at my watch, but I did not register what time it was.

The very gesture was a desperate effort to not draw attention to myself, to impose order from chaos that lies within my own mind. My fingertips made contact with the metal in my pocket again and again, both comforting and disturbing. I paused and shut my eyes and breathed in the damp air. When I opened them, he was there.

Coming out of the pub's darkness, his black protégé was unmistakable. He moved with the same relaxed arrogance, the kind that had once made my blood boil. However, tonight I did not feel anger or the fury, uncontrolled rage that tormented me in the past. Tonight, I felt cold, calculating. Focused. He didn't see me at first, his attention focused on lighting a cigarette. The flame of his lighter momentarily cast a shadow over his face and I caught a glimpse of the barely perceptible wry smirk that traced the edges of his lips. The same smirk I'd seen that evening imprinted on my mind. My hand clenched around the metal in my pocket, the edges forcing into my palm. I stepped down from the lamppost, slowly, deliberately, foot by foot.

His gaze matched mine, I made contact with him before he did, and I turned to cross the road, and his gaze landed on mine. For a short time, the smirk evaporated, and something underneath appeared. Wariness. Recognition. Good. I cupped my arms and literally stopped a few feet away, allowing the space between us to expand. The street was empty, and the town noise was a dull hum. He took one puff of his cigarette, the flame briefly then darted for a second as a cloud of smoke came out. His stance changed, imperceptibly but obviously, to something ready to move, something sort of a challenge.

"You've got some guts," he mumbled, his voice almost a sigh. The words hung in the air, heavy with implication. I didn't respond. Words felt unnecessary, irrelevant. I allowed the weight of my own presence to speak for itself, the strength of my stare constant. His smirk returned, but it was thinner now, forced.

"What's the plan, then?" Scars asked, flicking ash onto the pavement.

"You wanting a square go?" The question lingered, taunting, but I still didn't answer. Instead, I took a small step at a time, narrowing the distance between us. He straightened, and the smile vanished again, and for the first time I saw something but a flicker of doubt in his eyes.

I never crossed the line to occupy his space, too close for him to perceive the level of anxiety emanating from my body. My hand remained in my pocket, the cold metal touching my skin. He saw the movement, his eye momentarily leaving mine, then looking back into mine. No longer was his smile gone, but replaced by a flicker of cold, a calculable thought.

"Be careful wee man," he cautioned, in a quieter tone, yet no less tense.

"You don't want to start something you can't finish." I crept closer and closer, with only the intention of moving my presence over him. The tension crackled like static electricity, the air between us was charged, brittle.

Then, without a word, I stepped back. The sudden movement broke the stare, and he drew in a sudden breath, inaudible, his shoulders barely moving. I left the front of the pub and walked back towards the alleyway, deliberately due to so many people being around, there can't be any witnesses. I didn't look back, but I could feel his eyes on me, burning into my back.

A message had been sent. He now knew I was coming. And that was enough. For now. There's a fine line between revenge and survival. Tonight, I'd taken my first step onto that line. And I had no intention of turning back.

The Ghost of
Tullichewan

The sharp scraping sound in my mouth, the sickening cracking sensation as the bone gave way, and the recoil of the pain that had already shattered my jaw. It had destroyed something beneath, the surface of which for me, might never recover. But until the time of the next meeting, I walked aimlessly and restlessly around the streets of Tullichewan, a phantom, without a purpose.

I went by the streets now bare of their comforting feeling, they no longer felt like home. Tullichewan felt too cramped, its streets too narrow to be functional in any useful way, as if I had turned my back on it or as if it had remained frozen in some way that I couldn't articulate. Once, I'd loved this place fiercely. Now, it felt tainted. The chipped tarmac, drug users and sagging fences bore the weight of years I didn't remember noticing before.

Nevertheless, it wasn't just the scheme that was changing, but also me. Taking long strides, my shoulders slumped, my fists nestled deep in my coat pockets, my muscle were tense, they felt ready to blow up at the slightest movement. At every step, it seemed to press harder down, motivating in pushing me headfirst into the inevitable. Sleep had become a rare and fleeting at the mercy of the earlier events. Night after night I tossed and turned, too defeated to get out of bed and finally just lay in the same space on the floor, until the walls seemed to close in.

The worst nights were the endless ones, were time seemed to get longer and longer to an almost horrific crawl. Whenever I could not cope with staring at the walls in the darkness, I would run off and follow the tracks of Tullichewan like a phantom black effigy, in a desperate call to it, to anyone, to someone. McColl Avenue, Craig Avenue, Taylor Street, these streets were not strangers, but old friends, just so gone. I walked them on a loop, through alleys and streets, over neglected pieces of land in a hypnotic shambling dance, thoughtless endless walking to try and tire myself out.

The council houses stood as steadfast witnesses, their weathered exteriors marked by peeling paint and cracked windows, staring blankly into the night. The scheme seemed to be holding its breath. The only sound was the intermittent engine noise of a car speeding on the A82 at the back of the scheme. In the dead of the night, I could pass undetectable, walking on the periphery of small whirlpool of light thrown by the few lamps dotted around.

The Bannachra Crescent playground lay at the side of some houses, a ghost of my childhood for what was there previously. It echoed in the sound of children laughing, in the screech of football boots hitting a wobbly goal frame. At night it was a bare scene, devoured by the long, creeping fingers of blackness.

The swaying motions switched back and forth gently through the wind, while the broken links of the gravel fence crackled softly. Walls graffitied with tags of defiance, temporary practices of rebellion that would inevitably wash away in the rain or be painted over in time. I rested against the fence, holding cool metal of the gates, and watched the empty play area. My thoughts slid backward, unbidden, into childhood. Those streets had once been alive with possibilities. The fights were now messy and no longer a bit of fun, ostentatiously painful but humorous. We thought we were invincible. But the brawls were no longer playful, and the laughter was replaced by the crying voice of the wind ripping through the branches and the low far cry of a train.

For the first time, I questioned if I had ever really loved Tullichewan, or if I had just been deliberately blind to what it had always been. The scheme felt heavy now, burdened by the collective anger and pain of its residents. Perhaps it had been this way all along and I had only now become aware of it. The sound of laughter, the glass on the bottle, an argument that goes on increasing until it ends, that falls silent. Walking along Cullen Street I trailed the dark paths around a fallen streetlamp, a circle of teenagers huddled close, their silhouettes lost in the shadows.

I wasn't seen as I went by, lost in the haze of their shared funny stories and the slight drunken state of the group. They evoked a strange awareness in me, a duality within my own consciousness a resemblance between the self I knew and the one I had become, shadowy and uncertain. My alternate persona had made me think of a complex mosaic, of another character, one who is irreverent, restless, and liminal. This new persona appeared split, trapped between this desire to escape the walls of the house and the great weight of responsibility for its upkeep. I wondered if maybe they too felt that same unrest brewing just under the surface. Maybe they did. Maybe, like me, they were just waiting for the world to light up the fuse.

When I made a turn from the road, I saw a person casually resting against a car. For a second a blindingly bright red light went out in the dark the moment, it was Paul as he took a hit off his cigarette and partially exposed his sharp countenance. He watched me approach and his eyes fixed with the subtlest smile or observation.

"Out and about early mate?" he rasped on a deep, bassy voice, smoke curling up like a serpent from his lips.

"Thought you'd have found him by now." he continued, I just shrugged it off, pretending that I couldn't fight the feeling of having found him already, ignoring the fact he expected an answer, hoping it would render the heaving of anger that had gotten trapped deep inside.

"He'll be there," I said, however it sounded empty, a deception to myself rather than him. Paul made another careful pull, coughing and exhaling deliberately, as if thinking ahead. His gaze cut into me, sharp and unyielding.

"You look like hell, are you sleeping?" Paul asked, the truth covering my entire appearance as stark as the resistance in my jaw muscles was, Paul winced, eyebrow creeping up, and the corner of his mouth involuntarily skipping a jump, into what wouldn't have been looking exactly on the side of a smile.

"Sure, you're not, are you. Listen, kid. You can't keep this up forever. I've been there, expecting a fight that seems to be forever out of reach. It'll eat you alive. You need to clear your head, or you're gonna lose before you, before you even get started." His words made my fists clench in my pockets. My tension constricted with each utterance as if a spring strained to its limit.

"I don't need to clear my head," I snapped.

"I know exactly what I'm doing." Paul's smirk widened, but his eyes remained cold and calculating.

"Maybe you do. But if you are not careful this can cost a lot that you may not want to spend. I've seen it happen before." His speech was monotone, unemotional, without pity or a warning. During that short period, his utterance lingered between us, heavy and restrictive. I felt the pressure of them coming down on my shoulders, but I did not speak of it. I'd already decided, and it was game over.

Paul took a drag, and the cigarette ember blinked like a small, malevolent gaze in the dark.

"Just don't forget," he said, lowering his voice to a low, even tone,

"Once you step over that line, it can't be undone," respectively. I didn't respond. There was nothing to say. His voice resonated in my head and there, along with the sound that reached my ear in every footstep on the floor as I turned and walked on, every footstep, the danger would point to what he warned me about. The line he spoke of was ahead, a shadow on the horizon, but I'd known all along that I would cross it. However, I followed through on my intention and made sure that Scars understood the decision it would mandate.

The hours all blended and faded into the same endless loop of streetwalking and an unquiet mind. I couldn't help but let Paul's lecture linger in the back of my mind, a voice I couldn't quite drown out. But they couldn't extinguish the fire in my chest, that raw, searing anger that burned brighter with every passing moment. The memory of that night replayed in an ongoing loop in my brain, sharp and unrelenting. The cutting laughter of the scars, the hard steel biting the teeth of my jaw, the shooting pain of my jaw literally being broken it all unfolded before me, replaying again and again, crystal clear.

My fists would always tighten whenever the spinning reel came back and the simmering rage in my stomach would just keep building up and growing up. Sleep was a battlefield. The only time came, fleeting, and roving, marked by nightmares that would pull me back into the now. I'd wake drenched in sweat, my heart racing, fists curled so tightly my knuckles ached. Even in sleep, my body braced itself for the fight to come. On that evening, as a soft, constant rain fell, I went back to McColl Avenue.

The street was deserted except for the occasional glimpse of activity through the windowpanes, and the incidental glow cast by television sets. Rain pooled in the pavement, its hazy, orange streetlight shimmered and dripped down. The air was muggy and perfumed with damp earth and freshly placed concrete. the old playground on Bannachra Crescent. Rotary chains from the swings oscillated gently with the wind current and produced a soft clang thanks to the rust.

With the ground soaked by rain it became mud and became hard to walk through, the houses stood like wraiths in the darkness. I stood for a long time in the rain, letting my clothes saturate and looked into the abyss. The echoes of my childhood surfaced again faint and bittersweet. But a while back, the sound of trainers squeaking and cries of 'VICTORY' used to ring out on the grass field and gravel park of this scheme before they built the new houses. Now, it felt hollow, a monument to something I'd lost or maybe never had.

The rain grew louder on my jacket hood, the rain paralleled a steady beat on down on the march echo of every footstep. The streets were empty for the first time and only the rhythmic sound of my shoes in puddles filled the air and then thought I saw him. Someone crossed over at the other side of the street. The beat of my heart pulsated against the bone of my ribcage and adrenaline flooded my arteries. He stood there, perfectly relaxed, almost nonchalant, but something about him ignited my internal alarms. He was waiting. Watching. I froze, my breath catching in my throat. The streets washed away by the rain, and I wiped the rain from my face, but I could only make out very slight facial features. Was it him? The figure stood there in silence, an oppressive feeling of unease spreading all around.

And just as he'd appeared, he disappeared, turning and fading back into the darkness, without a sound. For a moment, I stood rooted to the spot, my thoughts whirling.

I willed my legs to move and walk behind him, trainers splashing through puddles. The streets blurred and closed together around me, and all the mundane features of Tullichewan transformed into a disorienting, uncanny mirage.

I made the rounds up to a corner, and then another corner, looking into every shadow and every street, but he was no exception. I came to a sudden halt in the middle of the road, caught in sheets of torrential rain, anger building to a boil. Was it him? Or had my mind conjured him out of desperation? Wet to the bone I tightened my fists close by my sides, as the force of the storm rapped at the glass bus shelter in front of me, but it did not compare to the storm in my very core.

The waiting was consuming me whole. As I turned around to head home the rain washed out my footprint and the scheme stood there in stillness, its presence as comfortable as it was stifling. Tullichewan didn't forgive or forget. Neither did I. The fire in my chest refused to die. That momentary view of a silhouette had reactivated my bloodthirst. This wait was nearly over. One way or another, this would end. The next time I saw him, there would be no walking away and no hiding.

Restless

Another night, endlessly pacing the streets, the air felt heavy, thick with dampness, as if the sky itself pressed down on the streets of Tullichewan. Every breath seemed harder to take, every step dragged with a weight that had nothing to do with the weather. The scheme lay out in front of me, a collage of decaying council flats, lost lanes, and flickering lamps. It wasn't home not anymore.

It was a place I moved through, something I endured. I walked past a street of houses with sagging gutters and peeling paint. Offstage, dim blue lights emanating from televisions sometimes spilled through for a moment of desaturated spectacles. The occasional shout or muffled laugh broke through the quiet, reminders that life carried on, even in places like this. But it all felt distant, as though I were walking through a world just out of reach.

The streets themselves seemed alive in their decay, roads littered with potholes completely flooded with rainwater, the puddles cast a hazy orange shimmer off of the streetlights and weeds pushed boldly through broken pavements. A dented and rusty trolley lay derelict on its side by the entrance to an alley, with its wheels twisted, the final testament to a journey that now belonged to the past.

Scars, Just the idea of his name caused my jaw to clench, an absent pain which always seemed to linger. He was, to put it frankly, around the corner and the other side of the block of flats and his mate was coming to visit, an opportunity in ways I could not ignore. I didn't know when I'd cross paths with him again, but it was certain I would. But the time for that would arrive, and it would be one of two ways, an arranged meet or Scars getting picked and tied up by Mick and Paul.

When I rounded the corner, I saw a line of boarded up garages set for demolition, covered with graffiti and dirt.

EVERYONE LEAVES

was scrawled in thick black paint across one of the garages. I paused for a moment, staring at the words. They felt like a truth too bitter to swallow. Not everyone leaves, I thought. Some of us stay. There are others that are effectively undefeatable, regardless of how much we might want to flee. A car drove by its tires splashed through a puddle soaking the curb and me with it. I wasn't able to react in time, the numb cold penetrating water soaked between my skin and the callous denim. The driver didn't even glance back. I flailed at my leg more out of anger than anything else and enraged I kept walking.

The farther I walked, the quieter it became. The ambience of faraway tv noise and muffled talk disappeared as the murmur of wind passing through the narrow streets filled the void. The scheme always felt different at night.

Daytime was a busy buzz of children on bicycles navigating traffic, people chatting across garden walls, the occasional bark of a dog. But at night, it became something else entirely. The scheme became oppressive, punctuated only by a tapping of a tin can rolling down the empty road or by the receding growl of a train building up in the distance near Rosshead. I stopped at the edge of the football park, little more than a patch of overgrown grass surrounded by a rusting fence and fully enclosed by houses and flats.

A single bench sat beneath a crooked streetlamp, its surface scarred with knife marks of earlier menchies and fading bombers scorched into the wood. I stopped, then sat, and my weight landed on the yielding boards. For a moment I closed my eyes and let the air engulf my skin. Memories came unbidden, sharp, and vivid. I just thought about all the brawls we used to get into around here with the guys, drunken laughs carrying on with the young team. Rather than genuine fights that could have injured, playful bouts that boys did to test the limits of their strength. Back then, we thought we were invincible. But that was a long time ago. I opened my eyes and brought myself forward, resting my arms on my knees, looking at the ground. The luminance of the lamp post was low, and it produced long shadows over the park.

I mused whether sitting in this very spot, Scars had always gazed at the same gloomy outlines. Had he felt what I felt now? The pull of something dark, something inevitable? All of a sudden, I felt the shivers down my spine, and I reached up to stand, pushing my hands down into the pockets of my coat and pulling them out. I couldn't sit here any longer. I needed to keep moving, even if I didn't know where I was going. The breeze grew stronger as I ambled, pulling at my coat and scattering the contents on the road.

The sound of my footsteps echoed faintly, the only sign of life on the empty streets. I was now at the old phone box, its Perspex panes dirty, opaque. Inside a phone number had been scribbled, and beside it,

FOR A GOOD TIME, CALL

I let out a small snort, a sound totally incongruous with the silence. Here, in this rundown place of Tullichewan, somebody had made a mark. Having drawn closer and closer to the border of the scheme my step quickened. Yet, lay the A82, a route to anywhere else. I got to the edge of the woods, viewing the road as cars whizzed by with headlights shining through the night. For a short while I contemplated what it would be like to abandon Tullichewan, to get in a car and just drive till Tullichewan became a mere memory.

But I couldn't leave. Not yet. Not while Scars was still out there. Going back through the woods my movements careful with the slippery ground underneath, I retraced my steps back to the scheme, with the wind in my favour, pushing me ahead. An enormous weight of the future settled upon my back, but I wasn't crushed. Not tonight. The wind carried a faint smell of rain as I wound my way back through Tullichewan's streets.

Night fell and over the hills on either side twilight fell, save for the soft glow from the moon illuminating the distant windows of a few houses' miles away. My steps echoed faintly, a solitary rhythm in the emptiness. I wasn't quite sure how long I'd been walking, but it didn't matter. Time seems to have been stretched and bent time in on itself all week, each second the same as the next. I knew that the more I displaced, the more hushed they sounded, became, albeit slightly.

Something soft rustled and I quickly turned around, heart thumping against my ribs. A fucking cat came out of the back of a skip, its eyes glinted, in the time of shimmering light, and it disappeared into the darkness. I exhaled slowly, the tension in my chest easing. Paranoia began to build, infiltrating all areas of my thoughts. I saw Scars in every shadow, I heard his voice in the moan of the breeze. It felt like the house itself, a conspiracy, was there to play on my fear and keep me on edge, the twists and turns in the narrow streets and corners bearing the threats of the night.

I came to a stop on the edge of a deserted car park, the concrete cracked and wet let off a sheen from the damp. Highlighted more from by the glow off of a streetlamp, a tentative ray of light spilled over the parking lot. In an instant I stayed motionless. He'll show up when he's ready, I thought. Scars wasn't the kind of man you found. He was the kind who found you, lurking just out of sight until the moment was right. I actually hated that I knew this about him, hated that he took up so much room in my head. But there was no denying it. Scars had a way of making himself unavoidable.

I followed the trail back and continued on, my feet moving quickly without the target in mind. The scheme grew quieter as the night moved on, the kind of quiet that felt like it was holding its breath.

Occasionally the sounds of something in the distance, or the screech from bats were interspersed through the quiet, however they were transitory and disappeared back into the darkness of the night very quickly. The idea of coming back to the flat floated by my head, but I pushed it aside almost as soon as it came up. The notion of being in isolation in my flat with only my thoughts for company was unbearable. Here, at the very least, I was free to imagine myself searching for an something with more meaning.

When I stepped into another street an unknown figure came up against the lamppost just down the road. The light of a cigarette in the air illuminated his face for a moment and then it was hidden under a haze of smoke. Was it Paul. He then made himself known

"Out again," he murmured, I recognised his husky voice and grating as I came close.

"Can't sleep," I replied, the words coming out before I even realised, I'd spoken to Paul. He grinned spitefully and his pupils constricted as he watched me.

"You look like it." He gestured with the cigarette, the ember flaring.

"You're gonna burn yourself out if you keep this up." I shrugged, the motion automatic, now getting bored of his lectures, even though he may care about me and looking out for my best interests.

"I'm fine." I replied back,

"Sure, I bet you are," Paul said, his tone unreadable. Taking another drag, and the smoke drifted up before it went out of sight.

"You're wound tighter than a snare drum. Let me guess still waiting for him to show?" Paul knew my intentions, I nodded, my jaw tightening. Paul exhaled slowly, his eyes never leaving mine.

"You know he's not just gonna walk up and make it easy for you, right? That's not his style. We'll pick him up" Paul reassuring me this time, that he and Mick had it covered.

"I know, I can't sit idle" I said, my voice clipped. Paul got to his feet and flicked the cigarette onto the tarmac and then stepped on it.

"Good. Just make sure you're ready when the time comes. And don't just let him get you so worked up. He's already taken enough from you." I didn't respond. What was there to say? Paul was right, but releasing the simmering anger and the desire to be always prepared was not simple. Paul sighed, shoving his hands into his pockets.

"Go home, kid. Get some rest. You'll need it." I watched as he walked away, his figure disappearing into the shadows. For a brief period, I froze in place, taking everything in and then surrendered to now turn around and go back towards the flat.

Tonight, felt wasted and Paul's words, fell on my shoulders heavy, but the weight could not damper my thirst for revenge. The moment I got to the flat, the sky changed abruptly. The gentlest of morning light applied itself to the sky, a subtle, wavering gleam of a cloud more fleeting than air. It was the last of the night, but not a time to get comfortable. I reached the door and hesitated, my hand resting on the handle.

Inside the flat was cold, impersonal, but it was the last place still possible to get some sort of rest. I entered, and the sound of the door closing as the room fell silent before I closed it. The room was as I'd left it bare, stark, with only the essentials. A battered chair sat in the corner near the window, its upholstery torn in places. In front of it sat a rather small table with an empty glass and a bottle with the last dregs of whisky in it.

I slumped onto the chair, supine with my flexed elbows on knees. My gaze drifted out the window, the scheme outside bathed in the faint blue light of early morning. The anger simmered beneath my skin, restless and unrelenting. The waiting was terrible, but I knew it wouldn't take much longer.

Scars was out there, somewhere, and he would get his. Don't let him live in your head rent free, the last of Pauls words running through my mind. Although that was Easier said than done. For now, all I could do was wait and I was getting impatient. But, when the first beams of sunlight touched the roof in the early hours of the morning, I felt a calm before the storm.

The Calm

The street was eerily still, as if it were aware of what was going to happen and had decided to keep its mouth shut. We were in Fraser Avenue, nestled in the heart of Dumbarton's residential sprawl near Bellsmyre, it was a patchwork of older stone terraces and some post war wooden homes. The houses huddled in close confined ranks, their aged pebbledash exteriors giving off an impression of perpetual dark. Even the thin strips of gardens between the pavement and front doors seemed to have resigned themselves to neglect, overgrown with weeds and littered with remnants of lives once more hopeful.

This was a legacy of time, aged by decades of use and neglect. The single streetlamp above sputtered intermittently, casting a jaundiced glow onto the cracked pavement below. The light converged in patches around the road was unsmooth, scattered by the gaunt outlines of some almost dead trees, planted alongside the curb. Their gnarled branches reached out like bony fingers, grasping at the dewy air. Roots broke through, emerging up through the pavement, a rebellion against its confined space, nature fighting back, weaving a warped, it was jagged under the sole of my shoes.

The smell of night was heavy of wet stone and moss, a soft, slightly damp, mustiness that settled on everything like a blanket. The air carried the damp chill, seeping into my lungs. I was slung low behind a hedge of unkempt borders of one of the council builds, I touched the ground below me, yielding and musk of decay. The hedges were overgrown, the branches protruding at random angles, testimony to neglect for years.

Below me was fragments of a broken glass, a beer bottle perhaps, it gave off a muffled crunch, a reminder of a good evening perhaps that been had of another night. Across the street, his house sat among a row of identical builds, each one a tired reflection of its neighbour. A rusting bicycle leaning against the wall, a rose bush just too thick to maintain grew around a window, a cracked garden gnome standing guard over a dark staircase. It was a place time seemed to have forgot, a routine where the ambition had solidified into automatism. Dreams had withered and cracked like the pavement.

The police station stood behind his house, down by the A82 in the shape of a monolithic object, cast its shape in a cold light that diffused in the soft darkness of the outside. It was big enough to be observed, yet too distant to be relevant, its mere presence more iconic than useful, a passive witness that would not act. The occasion hum of idling vehicles or the sharp crackle of a dispatcher's voice broke the stillness, but the words were faint and meaningless. The silence would always come back, the only other interruptions were the distant bark of a dog or the low tone of people talking seeping out through the flimsy walls.

A curtain moved in a neighbours' window across the street, the movement so fleeting it could well have been missed. No face appeared. The night swallowed it whole, leaving the house in darkness once again. Down the street on Argyle Avenue, the van waited parked, its engine off, hidden between an abandoned car with flat tires and another van. The grime on their window and the mould clinging to their edges suggested they hadn't moved in weeks.

The positioning of the van was not accidental, but rather deliberate, and camouflaged by a hedge of trees. Inside, Mick and Paul waited in silence, the tension palpable even from here. This plan had been rehearsed to exhaustion. Every aspect was engraved in my memory, but tonight, it was different, there was something austere to it, something final.

The damp air pressed against my skin, mingling with the quiet hum of the distant River Clyde as it wound its way past Dumbarton outward onto Helensburgh. The night hummed with a charge, a tension that fuelled the resolve that burned in me. a place where neighbours exchanged nods and kids chalked hopscotch lines on the pavement. But by night, it transformed. Shadows deepened, silence intensified, and cracks in its face no longer could be ignored.

Across the street, the outline of an old stone church stood against the murky sky, its steeple barely visible in the darkness. Once a symbol of faith and hope, its stained-glass windows cracked, holes in the roof tiles and its cobblestones overrun with weeds. Weatherboarded, and left to fester, the church stood on its own ground as if inquisition, its emptiness more resonant than even a sermon.

I considered taking Scars also for a walk inside that church, making him to stand in front of its soullessness, its desolation. Give him the sensation of the night bearing down on him like it once did on me for so long. This wasn't going to be quick or clean. What lay ahead tonight was going to be planned, a reckoning long overdue. An airy crunch of footsteps snapped me out of my contemplation. I turned my neck just a bit to see Paul and Mick walking towards me in the dark. Their movements were quiet, practiced.

Mick's broad shoulders and dark cap blended seamlessly into the night, while Paul's wiry frame carried a sharp energy, his gaze darting around with restless focus. They crouched down by me speechless, the tension between us as real as my own. I glanced at them briefly. No words were needed. We were ready.

"Did anyone move?" Mick said, using a low, gruff voice, hardly a whisper. I shook my head, gaze fixed on the house.

"Lights went off about an hour ago. He hasn't come out since." I replied.

Paul moved closer; his face bathed in the soft light of a streetlight on the opposite side street.

"So, what's the play? Straight in through the front?" I shook my head again, my eyes moving along the darkened street.

"No. We wait. If he goes out to smoke, we grab him, though. Otherwise, we go in via the back. Quiet. No fuss. No attention." Paul agreed, but not before I detected a glimpse of nervousness in his gaze. He didn't say anything, and I didn't press him. Mick remained silent, his focus unyielding.

He thrived in these moments, right before the action, when every movement and thought carried weight, carried consequences. Every Passing second seemed to drag, each one stretching into an eternity. The damp air pressed in on me, the cold creeping into my knees, hard against the earth.

Somewhere in the distance, a dog barked sharply before falling silent. At last, I showed the nod to Mick to assume the agreed position. He vanished into the darkness, moving along the side of the house with purpose. Paul and I hunkered down, crouched, watching the house and the street, silence bearing down like a physical pressure on both of us. Paul and I crouched low, the damp seeping into my knees and creeping through the fabric of my jeans.

The house now in front of us, it was still dark and silent, with empty windows, we were peering into the dark rooms. A short distance in front, I caught the vague outline of Mick's movement, only just in the evening mist. He was set up now, against the side gable wall, watching the back door. Paul shifted beside me, his movements subtle but deliberate. His fingers made a barely perceptible contact against his thigh. It was a habit I'd noticed before, something he did when the waiting stretched too long, and the tension gnawed at his nerves. I glanced at him, catching the faint outline of his face in the dim light. His jaw was tight, his gaze fixed on the house. That lingering uncertainty I'd caught in passing is gone, instead of it was replaced by the unflinching cold calculation that has enabled us to survive as many nights as this.

"You think he's asleep? Paul whispered, his voice low and steady."

"Possibly," I replied, my eyes never leaving the front door.

"But we're not rushing this. We wait for Mick's signal. If he moves, we move." Paul made a little affirmative nod and went back into the cover of the hedge. He put me in charge, and so I put Mick on guard, just as I trusted Mick to keep an eye on me. It was an intuitive sense, arising through shared experience close collaboration in the face of crisis.

The minutes dragged, stretching longer with each passing second. The street was eerily quiet, each sound magnified by its absence. A car purred in the background, its engine a whisper in the distance. A breeze stirred the hedges, the rustling leaves sounding almost deafening in the absence of anything else. From where I stood, I could almost make out the ghostly outline of the police station down the street, its cold fluorescent light slicing through the night like a scalpel. It wasn't close enough to pose an immediate threat, but its presence was a constant reminder of the fine line we walked.

Even a single misstep, a single fall, and it's over, the whole thing evaporates in the blink of an eye. I bent my fingers and felt the stiffness at my knuckles from my previous battles. As we waited the memory of that night lingered, Scars' twisted grin, the sickening sound fists connecting with my flesh, and then rush of adrenaline had surged through me.

But tonight wasn't about messages or warnings. Tonight was about closure. The door creaked open, its hinges sighing in the hollow soundlessness. Someone is coming out, a dark shape in front of the weak light of the lamp post at the end of the road. My breath held captive when I saw him walk up to the end of the garden. He was wearing a heavy jacket, the collar of the jacket pulled up high to keep out the cold and his hands by his waist. His movements were unhurried, almost careless, like he had all the time in the world. It was him. My heart thumped against my ribs, with every beat a drum in my ears as I pored my eyes onto Scars. His face was older, the years etched into his features, but there was no mistaking him. More Scars surrounded his mouth, the old scar just above his cheek, and the way it moved was all imprinted in my mind.

The cold hard metallic inside my mouth, the malic laughing that had been torturing my brain, the freshness of blood in my mouth. When Pauls hand touched my arm it yanked me into it, his hold firm but sure. It was a still moment of the urge to hold my feelings in. I nodded, inhaling deeply to steady myself. My breath fogging in the cold ambient air, I attempted to draw Mick's attention. Arm in arm we emerged from the darkness, onto the pavement's edge in front of the breathing luminous cloud of the earlier breath. Scars body froze mid drag, the cigarette dangling from his lips. His eyes flicked toward us, narrowing as recognition dawned. For a fleeting moment he stood stationary, like a deer in the headlights, was he ready to flee or to wage war.

"Evening fuck face," I said, my voice low and even. The cigarette fell from his lips onto the paving slabs leaving a soft hiss as the ember went out in the wet pavement. His gaze flitted back and forth between me and Paul, and finally to Mick, who had inexplicably appeared behind him, blocking any escape.

"What… what the fuck do you want?" he stammered, his voice shaky, betraying the fear he tried to hide. I stepped closer, my movements deliberate, each footfall measured.

"I told you I was coming for you." I said, my tone calm but sharp enough to hint at what was to follow. His stare wavered, colour draining from his face as the dots connected.

"I… I didn't… he began, but the words stuck in his throat, swallowed by the weight of the moment. I stopped just a small distance off were he stood, where I could observe the shimmer of sweat run down his forehead even in the coldness. His hands shook slightly, and I could see the subtle upswings and downswings of his chest with each breath becoming faster.

"You didn't think I'd forget, or let you away with what you had done to me, did you?" I asked, my voice quiet but laced with venom. He began to speak but not a sound escaped. His wide, imploring eyes scanned among the three of us in search of an exit. I made one more step in the direction of us getting closer and closer together.

"Not here," I said, glancing at Mick. Mick nodded, stepping forward to grab Scars by the arm. He knew he had no chance and did not fight back, Mick struck him on the back of the head and his body fell limp as Mick and Paul dragged him to the van. I followed behind, we made sure our footsteps were quiet on the street. The van slid door open, a low slap on the van floor, and we returned to the stillness. The rest of Scars was shoved inside, his breathing ragged and uneven.

Paul got in following him, his movement deliberate and purposeful, while Mick and I hung out for a moment in the street, making sure no one had witnessed what we had just done. The street was still, the light of the streetlamp forming its long shadows upon the pavement. I retraced my steps and went back to the house, its dark closed windows empty and bleak, I made sure we left nothing behind.

For all the world it was just a typical night in Dumbarton. Nevertheless, for Scars it was just the start of his slippery slope. I returned to the van and got inside shutting the door, which fell heavy with a resounding thud.

The Storm

Mick had strapped him in the back of the van, his wrists wrapped tight in coarse rope, with duct tape across his mouth. His eyes darted wildly when he came round, flicking from the rearview mirror to Paul, who was seated beside him, before finally locking onto me whenever I turned back from the passenger seat. His fear was unmistakable now, oozing through the thinning veneer of defiance he clung to like a drowning man grasping at driftwood.

On the road, the glow of Dumbarton streetlights swooped by in blobs of washed out yellow and orange, fading the world into a haze as Mick built the momentum. The houses of Fraser Avenue were well behind us, completely engulfed by the dreary, repetitive nature of the A82. The town's weary expansion disappeared altogether, being replaced by the emptiness of the straight road. In the rearview mirror, the flash of headlights from passing cars punctuated the growing darkness, each burst, a reminder that the world outside was still in motion. Inside the van, though, time seemed to crawl, each second drawn taut like a bowstring.

Paul sat rigid beside Scars, his arms crossed tightly over his chest, a picture of deliberate menace. His body angled subtly toward our guest like a silent warning, a promise of what might happen if he made the wrong move. He did not have to speak a word; his mere appearance was a danger by itself.

His lack of blinking, how he leaned just a little into scars so as to take up Scars personal, was just another poignant aspect of the silent intimidation. The sound was, at best, that of a persistent engine noise, occasionally punctuated by the low hum of the wheels rolling on the road surface. We all had not spoken since we had driven off from Fraser Avenue. There was no need. Every detail of this night had been planned meticulously, rehearsed in silence until words felt superfluous.

Mick, as always, was the embodiment of focus. His hands gripped the steering wheel firmly, his knuckles white under the faint green glow of the dashboard lights. His gaze was always fixed on the road, sharp and hard but every now and then, just for a moment, his eyes shifted over to the rearview mirror a simple check that our companion was unharmed and compliant. Then his attention snapped back to the road ahead, his movements exacting and methodical. I caught myself turning back to look at Scars more often than I needed to.

He was hunched between Paul and the back window, his bound wrists resting awkwardly in his lap. The rope abrading like, scratched, raw meat on his flesh delivered crimson angry looking marks that brood with the jarring motion of the van. The duct tape clamping his mouth was slick, perfectly cured and his edges sealed in a way that was almost clinically immaculate, with no room for wishful thinking. His chest rose and fell in shallow, uneven breaths, each inhale sounding like it might break into a sob. His eyes betrayed him.

The defiant spark that had burned so fiercely in Dumbarton now was fading down, like a candle being blown out by a gust of a draft. I could see the calculations behind his stare, the frantic weighing of options that dwindled with every mile we put behind us. The overhead lights thinned out as we got near to the Stoney Mullen Roundabout, their ugly light bleeding away into the overwhelming night. Mick took the left exit, guiding the van onto Upper Stoney Mullen Road. Uncomfortably it was a tight, winding bit of path that squeezed its way up into the hillsides, on both sides smothered by the thickets of trees. Their skeletal arms projected over the pavement toward the road, quieting and swaying in the night breeze like hungry shadows, telling us secrets that resisted touch.

The incline forced Mick to slow, the van's engine straining faintly against the climb. The road ahead curved sharply, its edges invisible in the blackness that seemed to devour everything beyond the reach of the headlights. Paul broke the silence on a low note, laced with a biting irony.

"Enjoying the ride?" he asked, leaning forward slightly.

Scars breathing hitched audibly, but he didn't respond. His gaze darted quickly from Paul to me, returning, before landing once more on his wrists in the restraints. Paul smiled, a barely noticeable sparkle in his eyes.

"Didn't think so," Paul muttered, leaning back again, arms still folded across his chest. The road narrowed further, the trees pressing in tighter. Their cast shadows slid out deep and sinuous along the side of the hood of the van, a nearly flowing blackness that rose and fell with the dance of the headlights. Through the occasional break in the foliage, I caught glimpses of Loch Lomond far below a sprawling void under the moonlight, its surface black and impenetrable. It would have been a breathtaking thing, by day a deep, blue, shimmering expanse as far as the eye could see. Yet beneath an overhang of night, it was no longer that, but a bottomless scar on the world, a phantom weight in my struggling chest.

Creak of the tires on the bumpy road surface, the distant rustling of leaves above, and Scars laboured breathing. I unconsciously clenched and unclenched my fists, the rough surface of my knuckles providing a tactile cue for the struggle that had brought us to this point. We saw a darkened farmhouse to the right, the house looked lifeless. One wispy thread of smoke drifted lazily from the top of the chimney, the only activity. Further along the way, a bed and breakfast rose up from the gloom. Its varnished wooden sign swayed slightly in the breeze, its letters faded and forgotten. The driveway was empty, the windows dark. It was a place left behind by the previous guest, much like this stretch of road, a relic of something that no longer mattered.

Mick glanced at me, breaking the silence with a single, measured statement.

"We're close," he said, his voice low, steady. I made a nod, and my eyes went to the back seat passenger again. His chest now rose and fell faster, and the painful truth of it all settled in. The comfort of Dumbarton the noise, the crowds, the illusion of safety was far behind us. Here, in the hills, cold and silent he was completely cut off and left alone. The road went steeply uphill once more, requiring Mick to increase the accelerator. Each turn was very slow and deliberate, riffing the van slightly with each turn.

Paul shifted in the floor of the van; his body coiled with the same tension that knotted my stomach. At last, the trees broke apart revealing a small gravel pit in the roadside. Mick parked it on the side of the road, the tires making a soft sound as the van came to a halt. He cut the engine, and the silence that followed was deafening, pressing in around us like a physical weight. There were only the soft ticking of the cooling engine and the rustling of the wind through the trees. Mick leaned back in his seat, exhaling slowly.

"This is it," he murmured. Paul and I stepped out first. The night air stung me like a slap, cold and sharp on my body. For a moment, we moved as though Scars in the back seat wasn't even there, stretching our legs, taking in the scene. The loch lay spread out beneath, its surface basking in the faintest of rays of moonlight. All around us, the forest rose, silent, and its peaks seemed to stretch out dreamily, morphed into beings.

Paul moved quickly to the back of the van. The loud crack of the door wrenching open penetrated the silence, and I heard the Scars inside jump from the noise. Paul pulled him hard by the arm, dragging him out with the brutal indifference bordering on cruelty. Scars stumbled, his knees buckling slightly, but he caught himself. When he lifted his gaze, his eyes blazed with a defiant emotion, but it was weak now, threadbare. He was beginning to understand.

Paul held tight to his arm so that his knuckles turned white with restrained pressure. He nearly fell over on the uneven gravel because of the blow to the head and his hands being bound, which quivered as if by instinct to compensate him. His stare flickered from Paul, Mick, and me, looking for a vulnerability, an escape route that he could take advantage of. But he found none. Mick took steps, measured, around the van, and his boots caused a virtually soundless crunch on the gravel. He walked with the purposeful stillness of a stalking animal that has already assessed and figured out that its target is trapped. His arrival was an aura in the air, heavy and inescapable. The man, in a state of agitation, began to breathe in increasingly forced and short gasses, but despite it, Scars did not utter a single word.

The moonlight, however, effectively diffused only slightly through the dense canopy above us, which broke the silhouette of the clearing. The loch glistened in the distance, a black canvas of water endlessly waving in the night. The trees beside us swayed gently in the breeze, their limbs softly creaking, like deformed, painful joints. Mick came to an abrupt halt a mere foot from Scars, his face a mask of impassiveness. He didn't need to speak; the quiet authority he exuded did all the talking. His posture wilted slightly, his shoulders sagging under the weight of the moment, though his lips remained taped, a flicker of defiance still clinging to him. I moved closer, my boots scooting on the gravel and now his stare flickered over to me.

Unevenly superimposed upon his fear, and with unyielding unwillingness to give way, it squeezed an icy feel out of my own breast.

"You're still holding onto it, aren't you?" I queried, my voice sharp as a knife through the quiet. It is that tiny spark, that inner voice saying, 'there's a way out'.

"Just say the right thing, make the right choice and everything will be okay," I Continued. He didn't respond. His jaw clenched, his bound hands shivered just a little, as the knot tighter and tighter on his wrists. I stepped again, observing the fissures in his resistance.

"You won't," my tone soft but laced with steel. This is not something you can just get out of by arguing or pleading. Paul removed the tape and the hold of Scars hand, quite suddenly with a violent push on him, he forced him back into a crumbing state. He stumbled over his own two feet, his wrists bound in a way that let alone paced by unsteady legs. Straightening he squared his shoulders, his look defiant yet unsteady.

"Is that supposed to scare me?" He mumbled; his sound rough but strong enough to contain a slither of insolence.

Mick let out a low chuckle, humourless and cold. He matched him and, in that moment made a deliberate snap on each step, his hand reached out with an uninterrupted pull of his clothing. The fellow's body leaped in front of Mick, exhaling a sudden sharp breath in through the clenched teeth. "You fucking scared yet?" Mick whispered, a voice low and hard. Scars didn't dare reply right away, his lips furrowing into a ghastly, quivering line. His eyes wandered among us, pausing, first at Mick's calm, unresponsive features, and then settling at my own.

"You," he said finally, his voice a low rasp, hoarse from fear or anger I couldn't tell.

"And what about it," I replied, taking another step closer. Recognition flickered in his eyes, followed quickly by disbelief and then something darker, guilt, maybe, or regret. The rate of his breathing accelerated and the resistance in his eyes caved, that is, failed to hold, like the thinnest ice yields to pressure.

"I didn't think you had it in you," he stammered, his voice cracking.

"I didn't..."

"Didn't what?" I flared in, my tone cutting through his justifications.

"Didn't mean to break my jaw? To leave me sprawled in a room, dripping in blood? Or didn't think I'd remember you?" His mouth opened in apparent protest, but no sound left it. The ensuing silence was crushing, the burden of his sin smothering the clearing like a sheet.

"Sorry," he managed at last, his voice little more than a gurgle.

"Sorry?" Mick repeated, his voice a low growl.

"Sorry doesn't fucking cut it." Paul stepped forward, his hands stuffed casually into his pockets, but his posture radiated threat.

"You don't get to 'sorry' your way out of this," he said, his tone almost conversational.

"Not this time." I approached step by step, until I was standing within a foot of him. Now his breathing was shallow, his chest rising and falling in panic.

"You'll remember this night for the rest of your life," I said, my voice calm, deliberate.

"Every word, every second. This isn't about me getting even. Above all, that you have an idea of the feeling of helpless and having no control whatsoever over what happens to you." Mick climbed into the van and grabbed more rope and a pole. His movements were slow, deliberate and gave Scars the time and chance to take in everything that was going on.

"Turn around," Mick said, his voice flat and emotionless. The man stopped, trembling, but then went on, after a moment of silence. Mick tied the rope deftly around his bound wrists, the motions so precise they bordered on mechanical.

"Come on," Mick said, pointing at the way in the woods. He paused, his brain darting to the left and right side, searching for a lifeline, some unspoken grace from one of our expressions. He found none.

"Fucking start walking," Mick repeated, his voice like stone. The man hesitantly walked forward staggeringly, his gait unsteadies, and every foot fall broken with the gravel giving way under his boots. We crept silently behind, on the meandering road down into the forest. Branches above the trunk swayed continuously in response to the breeze, and in doing so they did double duty, shifting the ground into fluctuating, membranous shapes.

By the time we got to a little opening in the edge of the pathway, Mick made a halt. He stood before us, his chest heaving, his visage white as a sheet in the moonlight.

"This is where it ends," I said, stepping forward. His breathing became unnaturally irregular, as his eyes jumped back and forth erratic between the two of us.

"Please," he stammered, his voice breaking.

"You don't have to do this. I... I Can make it up to you."

"How the fuck are you going to make it up to me" I interrupted.

"That's the only thing you have?" Mick retraced his steps, the coil of rope in his hand. You'll be able to remember this, he exclaimed, his voice even and low.

"Every detail." He cast the rope toward Paul who pulled it hard, dragging Scars along the slope of the hill. The ground went down abruptly to the steep hillside, the fall made more by thick weeds and undergrowth and a dark menacing shadow.

"Pick up the pace," Mick said, his voice leaving no chance for demurring. He was hesitant, trembling violently now. His eyes flitted back and forth between the drop, the dark and us. His bound hands made his movements awkward, his footsteps uneven as he made his way through the darkness. We stood in silence, listening to the sound of the woodlands surrounding us.

Reckoning

The forest felt alive a tight, suffocating tangle of shadow and secrets. The silence pressed down like a weight, thick with anticipation, as if the very trees held their breath and watched. Pale moonlight pierced the foliage, striking the ground and creating broken, jagged outlines in the wet, cool light.

With every footstep we sank a little deeper into the soil, making imprints in the soft ground, we had gone far out, far enough that if someone were in trouble they wouldn't be heard. This place was chosen, it was isolated, deliberate. Nothing would lead anyone here, this late at night. Even if someone did stumble upon us, it would mean they had intended to.

Tonight though, no such chance existed. Ahead of me, Mick shoved Scars forward. The force of the shove made him stumble forward, surprised by a resilient root shooting out of the ground. He righted himself without a word, his silence deliberate. Whether it was pride or calculation, I couldn't tell. The absence of protest was unnerving a vacuum that grew heavier with each step we took deeper into the forest.

Skeletal trees contorting against the dark sky, their distorted shapes exaggerated by the silvery gleam. Branches swaying in the wind came through resonated, as if the woods, bated their own longing to hear something. Paul trailed behind slowly, his footsteps deliberate and purposeful. His eyes locked on Scars; his expression was unyielding.

Mick, ahead, appeared almost casual, his movements loose and unhurried. But I knew him too well. Below the placid surface ran a keen whit of purpose. That was not the same kind of feeling, and not even Mick could completely hide it. Scars didn't look back. His hunched shoulders, tense and rigid, betrayed his restraint. He kept moving, his gaze darting sideways every so often, searching. There was no escape, not here. The forest was a cage of tangled roots and scattered detritus a broken landscape of twigs, leaves, and fallen branches. Even Scars seemed to realise that.

However, he did not give up, his defiance just below the surface. We reached the clearing, dominated by a massive oak tree that towered over its surroundings. Its old bark was gnarled and cracked; a guardian old tree that stood sentinel under the moonlight. Once Paul came to a stop, his keen eyes scanned the landscape then he nodded to Mick who replied with a terse grunt.

Mick grabbed Scars by the shoulder and shoved him toward the tree. Scars flew off the ground, bumping into the mighty bole of the oak. Mick didn't hesitate. He pressed him back against the rough bark with a force that brooked no argument. Paul approached and dragged a line of coarse rope from his shoulder. Together, they worked in eerie silence, looping the rope around Scars' chest and arms, binding him tight against the tree. The fibres bit into his skin, drawing a sharp grunt from him. He struggled, the ropes creaking under the strain, but he didn't resist outright. Mick took a step backward, looking at their handiwork with a discerning eye. Scars' forehead glistened from the sweat, his breaths coming fast and shallow. I got closer, the rumble of my boots against the wet ground a reminder of my intrusion. His eyes turned up to lock with mine, and for the first time I caught a glimmer of crack in the defiant wall.

"You thought you'd get away with it," I said, my voice low. The statements floated there, in a way that stung like one of a knife. He didn't respond, but his eyes betrayed him flashing with recognition, with fear. I leaned in closer.

"Not this time." In the clearing its sturdy oak was a solemn tomb, its deep trunk a witness to eternity. Scars, attached to its trunk, his stare burned into me, his face white and clammy with sweat. The space between us was thick, almost smother the air, saturated with the unvoiced fury and terror. His chest tightened as he fought the ropes, the sound of the ropes straining under his weight a ghostly creak in the air.

I stepped forward, the damp soil compressing beneath my boots. The cold, hard iron shaft was firm in my grasp. My grip tightened, each step bringing me closer to him, closer to the moment I had envisioned countless times since that night. Scars' gaze flicked from me to the bar, his lips parting as if to speak, but no words came. He was there to wait for mercy, there to wait for another postponement of the inevitable.

"Let's have no speeches tonight," I whispered into the wind, my words harsh in the stillness.

"You've had enough chances to explain yourself." His eyes widened, and his breathing grew shallow. He exerted much more force against the restraints, his body convulsing uncontrollably as if violence could be delivered to slip free. The oak bark complained as it yielded to his weight, but the knots Paul tied wouldn't loosen. His defiance had withered, replaced now by raw desperation. I swung the bar. The first blow landed across his side with a sickening thud, the impact reverberating through my arms. Scars screamed a guttural, broken sound that echoed in the stillness of the forest. He twitched against the ropes, his head thrashing back against the tree trunk. The churning scream rang in my ears, eclipsing all other sounds except his laboured breathing and the persistent throb in my arms from the blow.

Mick and Paul, now frozen in their place behind me, their bodies cast in the ghost of light coming through the leaves. This was my moment, and they knew it. No one intervened. Another swing. This time the bar connected with his thigh, and Scars howled, his voice shredding the quiet. His body contorted, but there was no way out, no possibility for escape. The lines scratched into his flesh, delivering painful reddened welts where they chaffed against his frantic undulating locomotion. I didn't stop. Blow after blow rained down his ribs, his shoulder, his legs.

Every hit was weighted, rhythmical, the bar a conduit for my rage. His cries turned to groans, then to whimpers, the fight draining out of him with every strike. His head slumped forward with trickling blood coming out of the mouth where the teeth had bitten his lip.

"You thought you'd walk away," I said, pausing for breath. My chest rose and fell with effort, my body, and especially my hand grasp, dripping with perspiration, all of them leaving a wet bar, slippery, uncomfortable, slick, and cold.

"That no one would come for you." He didn't respond. Couldn't. His head drooped and his body sagged against the ropes. Bloodstained his shirt in front dark and shiny in the weak moonlight. His respiration was shallow, irregular, his chest moving in spasmodic waves.

"You're going to carry this," I continued, stepping closer. My voice was now soft, almost sweet, yet powerful, bearing the weight of a vow.

"Every step, every breath you'll remember this night." I crouched to meet his gaze. His eyes, swollen and bloodshot, barely focused on me. But I saw it there the crack in his soul, the moment he realised there was no redemption here, no escape from the consequences of what he had done.

"Turn around," I said, grabbing hold of his face and lifting it. His face contorted in pain, but his gaze locked onto mine. For a moment, we were connected not as predator and prey, but as two broken men, bound by violence and hatred.

"Do you feel it now?" I asked, my voice a whisper.

"Do you understand?" He didn't answer, but the tears streaming down his face spoke louder than words ever could. I lifted his chin and set his head back down. The iron bar dropped from my hand, striking the floor with a soft sound, thud. Behind me, Mick and Paul remained silent, their presence a cold reminder of what had just transpired. The clearing was silent, the air heavy with the smell of blood and grime. The forest seemed to hold its breath, as if even the trees were recoiling from the brutality they had witnessed. I turned my back on Scars, and the sensation of night, crushing me.

"Untie him," I said to Mick, my voice flat, devoid of emotion. Mick hesitated for a moment but moved to the tree, his knife flashing briefly in the moonlight as he sliced through the ropes. Scars lay crumpled at his feet, his body now uncooperative and wrecked. He lingered there momentarily, coughing and wheezing, and then tried to move away.

"Fucking Go," I said, not looking back. My voice sounded the ultimatum of a sealed door, a final sentence without question of appeal. He didn't need to be told twice. Dragging himself to his feet, Scars shuffled in pain into the gloom, forming a fitful image against the devouring woods. His sobs faded into the distance, leaving only the rustling of leaves and the distant cry of an owl to fill the void. The forest was peaceful once more, like it was after some kind of violent storm. Not even the wind dared to stir. I stood there, staring at the spot where Scars had disappeared into the black maw of the trees, my breathing still uneven, my pulse pounding in my ears.

The iron bar lay at my feet, cold and useless now, like the carcass of something I'd killed. Mick cleared his throat behind me.

"He will return," he muttered, voice piercing the thick silence.

"Men like that always do." I didn't turn to look at him.

"Not tonight, he won't." Paul moved with uncharacteristic awkwardness, his boots landing with a crunch on the frost tilled earth.

"And if he does?" His voice wavered, uncertainty bleeding through the usual bravado.

"What then?" I bent down, picking up the bar. It became heavier that it used to be, its weight dropped into my palm, into my being.

"Then we finish it," I said.

"But for now, let's go." We got back into the forest, we three walked in silence. The trail we'd carved earlier looked different in reverse darker, more treacherous. The trees looked to descend further gnarled branches reach towards the ghostly oval of the moon light overhead. My legs felt heavy, each step dragging as if the earth itself wanted to hold me back. Paul broke the silence first.

"You think he'll tell anyone?" Paul asked.

"No," I said, my voice hard.

"What's he going to say? That the people he jumped came back to see him in the night. He'd rather crawl into a hole and die before admitting what happened." Mick grunted his agreement.

"If he survives." The words hung suspended, there but also unsaid, their meaning woven into the phrase itself. If scars survives, he may just bleed out in the woods, it wouldn't bother me. Not really. However, an itch at the borders of my cognition, a whisper I could not silence, nibbled away at the edges of my thought. Was I any better than him now?

The walk back through the forest felt lighter than I expected, almost as if the weight I'd carried for years had finally been lifted. The savoury scent of wet pine filled my lungs, cleaner now, no longer a burning ache of bitterness. My boots pressed firm against the soil with each step, the steady crunching beneath them marking the rhythm of my release. Ahead of me, Paul walked with his usual quiet confidence, the iron bar slung over his shoulder like it was nothing more than a tool of the trade. Mick trailed closely, his gait relaxed, his steps slow.

None of us spoke, and we didn't need to. I briefly looked back at the clearing we'd abandoned. The ropes hung limply to the trunk and swayed listlessly with the wind. The outline of Scars body was still to be seen, crouched on its base, contorted into himself. Sound of his pleading resonated softly in my mind no longer as a phantom memory but as a badge of victor. I had waited so long for this for the chance to take something back, to rewrite the ending of a story I never wanted to be part of.

When it was done, I did not feel regret. No doubt. Only a fierce, quiet satisfaction that settled in my chest like a steady flame.

"He didn't look so tough by the end," Paul said, his voice breaking the silence. He didn't turn around, but the faint curl of his words carried the same weight as his earlier actions.

"No, he didn't," I said, my voice calm, steady. Mick let out a low chuckle behind me.

"Sometimes it's not about how it starts," he said.

"It's about how it ends." And this, alas, had culminated exactly as it should have done. The woods seemed to taper off as we arrived, at which point the open sky above, a pale background with wisps of silver moonlight hung above. I could see the van parked where we'd left it, its dark shape blending into the shadows. The world beyond the woods felt distant, insignificant. All the important stuff had already occurred there, in the clearing beneath the belly of the oak trees. I was done.

This wasn't going to follow me any longer, wasn't going to prey on me as a stalker that I could never escape. Drawing close to the van Paul rests the iron bar against the van.

"You good?" he asked, his tone casual but his eyes sharp. I nodded, meeting his gaze.

"Yeah," I reply.

"I'm good."

"Right," Mick said, stepping out of the way and unlocking the van.

"Because we're not coming back here." I uttered a barely audible laugh, and it surprised me, even after the fact.

"No," I said, shaking my head.

"We're not." The three of us crammed into the van, the doors closing with a finality that felt right. When Mick fired the engine, the sound of its engine filled the silent of the night, a firm and stabilising hum. The road lay before us, the woods behind us shrinking on each second that crawled by. I pushed my back away from the seat and, for a second, shut my eyes. Replaying the events of that night, the violence, the laughter, the humiliation had always felt like a splinter under my skin, impossible to ignore no matter how much time had passed. But now? Now they felt distant, dulled. This wasn't forgiveness.

It wasn't redemption. It was justice, raw unforgiven vengeance, unflinching, and entirely mine. Scars in the clearing under the tree had seen it in my eyes. He'd known in every utterance, every movement, every strike. I had abrogated the power he stole, leaving him only with the emptiness of the naught he should have been as well as the marks we have branded on him.

The tires of the van screeched on the road, pulling away into the distance as Mick eased us back toward the A82 that had seemed so distant only a couple of hours earlier. Nevertheless, for the first time in long — time things weren't analogous to being preceded by the past. It was done. I opened my eyes and sighted the road ahead. The night was long and serene, but there was now a lucidity to it, a sharpness that there wasn't before.

For the first time, in a long time, I felt like I could breathe.

Printed in Great Britain
by Amazon

57819776R00148